James Garland

**Tregarthen Hall**

A Novel: Vol. II.

James Garland

**Tregarthen Hall**
*A Novel: Vol. II.*

ISBN/EAN: 9783337066406

Printed in Europe, USA, Canada, Australia, Japan

Cover: Foto ©Andreas Hilbeck / pixelio.de

More available books at **www.hansebooks.com**

# TREGARTHEN HALL.

# TREGARTHEN HALL.

A Novel.

BY

JAMES GARLAND.

*IN THREE VOLUMES.*

VOL. II.

LONDON:

TINSLEY BROTHERS, 18, CATHERINE ST., STRAND.

1871.

PRINTED BY TAYLOR AND CO.,
LITTLE QUEEN STREET, LINCOLN'S INN FIELDS.

# TREGARTHEN HALL.

—◆—

## CHAPTER I.

" So stately her bearing, so proud her array,
The main she will traverse for ever and aye."
WILSON, Isle of Palms.

LEAVING Power thus happily situated, the action of this story is here a little retroactive, and
is transferred to St. Keverne, where mine host
is busy with his customers, complaining with
them, or listening to their complaints at the bad-
ness of trade; that is, that smuggling had been
languishing of late. The 'Sylvia,' since she had
been at sea with her new commander, had been,
in their estimation, unusually and needlessly active in her duties. Rundlets were quite scarce
—scarcer than they had been for years, it was

quite difficult to get one for love or money.
Old Captain Dash declared he hardly knew
where to put his hand on one; and as to the
price, why, they were asking for one as much as
it was worth. Merlin had hitherto disappointed
their hopes; but now, however, they were aware
that there was likely to be a chance for them,
as the 'Sylvia' had been seen off the Land's
End very lately, and had not again made the
coast. St. Keverne was busy in expectation, as
the crews from the coves had been out fishing
for some time,—had, in fact, gone over to France,
and were going to make a run now,—that's what
all knew perfectly well, and were anxiously interested about. They had their opportunity, but
from no want of caution or foresight of the
'Sylvia.' Merlin had been guarding the coast
in his well-found cutter; the summer season had
departed, and October, with wintry winds, arrived. The wind had been blowing hard from
the south-east, quite fair for a splendid run from
the Land's End to the south of Ireland. Whilst
off the coast, Merlin was surprised, in the early
morning watch, at seeing coming round the
Land from the English Channel, a squadron
formed of a ship of the line and eight frigates.

He knew the position of the English Fleet, and his experienced eye told him they were French, although they had no bunting flying. His first question, "What are they up to?" being answered in his own mind, to the effect that they were bound for Ireland, and that another squadron had been fitted out, he had to lose no time in getting out of their way. They were between him and his country, and were sailing with about the same speed as himself. He saw that one of the frigates, by her peculiar proceedings, was selected to run his cutter down, or take her. True, the 'Sylvia's' pennant was lowered, which might cause her to escape notice as being a ship-of-war; but it had been seen, besides, the smart craft, with her taut rigging, told her history. Fortunately the wind freshened as the day drew on, with the incoming set of the tide from the great Atlantic. It was just the breeze that Merlin could get the most out of the 'Sylvia.'

"There is no help for it," he said, "we must run for it, or fight the frigate. She won't let me get back; she is to windward of me, and to cross her bows would be destruction."

"If this breeze lasts," said his lieutenant, "we shall be in Ireland in a few hours."

"Just so," said Merlin ; "depend upon it, their course is Bantry Bay, and they will drive me before them, to keep me from telling tales."

It was now quite clear why one frigate had been singled out; her sailing qualities were of a very high order, and but for the increasing wind and heavy seas—conditions most favourable for the 'Sylvia,' for she was a rough weather boat, and well she might be, for the coast she protected—she would have been very soon overtaken, because light winds and smooth seas for the frigate capable of spreading so much canvas, in royals and square lofty sails, necessarily caused her to glide through the smooth water at a great speed.

Merlin devoutly prayed for wind and seas, and at this time of the year it was probable that his prayer would not be disregarded. Great heavy clouds came rolling up from the west, causing the billows to rise very high.

"The frigate is gaining on us," Merlin was informed. It was true; a large shot from a 32-pounder was fired, and nearly fetched up to the cutter.

"She's about two miles from us," said Merlin, "and I fear I can't get away from her. We must fight to the death, and if I strike my flag, that moment I fire the magazine, and the 'Sylvia' sinks beneath the wild waves."

Loud cheers were the answer to this determination. Every man had his appointed duty, and calmly Merlin commanded his ship. Could she carry a gaft-topsail? Every windward rope was taut, and had its full strain; every wave coming in from the stormy Atlantic was considered. Some had to be resisted, the 'Sylvia' thereby keeping her position, and plunging through them; others had to be yielded to, as of too fierce a nature to withstand without relief; therefore ever and anon the word "Luff!" was passed aft to the steersman when the 'Sylvia' was to be helped, and "Steady!" when she had to meet the gusts of wind and wild waves in all their force. Another shot came up to the ship.

"She is gaining, Sir, and will rake us in another hour."

"I know it," said Merlin; "can nothing more be got out of the 'Sylvia,' Mr. Seabright?"

"Nothing, Sir; she is flying through the water like a bird in the air."

"I know it," coolly said Merlin.

Another shot came home, and struck the cutter, sending a shiver through her whole frame.

Merlin's blood was up now. The shot had struck his ship; another might hit his mast, and he would then be at the mercy of the frigate.

"Every man stand ready to cut away when ordered!" was bawled out by the boatswain.

"All ready!" "Ready, Sir!" "Bowse away!" The order was now given, and up went the gaft-topsail. "Luff!" was the only word spoken, and the dexterous steersman eased the ship and her mast when the sail was set, and received the wind. The mast quivered like a reed, the cutter groaned beneath her load, and was deluged in waves. Merlin was calm,—the mast had not broken, and had now become accustomed to its pressure. Merlin at length ventured to look over the taffrail, and in a moment he said,—

"If the wind last, Mr. Seabright, of which there is little doubt, and the topmast holds, the frigate will not fire another shot; we are gaining upon her, and we shall sleep in Cork to-night."

The frigate perceived the further press of canvas on the cutter, and confirmed Merlin's observation that the distance was greatening between them, as she now followed the course so successfully pursued by Merlin, and pressed on more canvas, but with an opposite effect. She was, as already noticed, a smooth-water ship, and a press of sail made her wet and roll, without accelerating her speed. She lost ground, and then reduced her sail as before. The distance gained was never lessened, and thus they continued until night came, when clouds and darkness obscured the horizon, but not until Merlin discovered that the race was abandoned, and the course of the frigate—and, as he surmised, the squadron also—was altered so as to weather Cape Clear, and either go into Bantry Bay, or around the western part of Ireland. Merlin pressed on, and early next morning he found himself in the Cove of Cork. He lost no time in writing his dispatch, which was of importance to the Government, for soon after the whole squadron was captured by Sir John Borlase off the west coast, and thereby the rebellion of Ireland was finally closed.

The news of a French squadron rounding Ireland, spread like wildfire throughout the south of the country. Extinguished hopes were revived, the wildest dreams were now to be realized. Men who had hid their faces for months, were now seen holding agitated conferences

with each other, making every preparation to
arm that was in their power, openly endeavouring to allure and seduce their countrymen to
join them.  Some few unreasonable enthusiasts,
unthinking and short-sighted patriots, were de-
ceived, and were added to their numbers; and
away in the mountains the green flag, with the
Irish harp on it, was hoisted.

Power heard of the movement with dismay;
Evered with delight.  He was ready to go to
the mountain, and follow the fortunes of the
down-trodden patriots, and have his name sung
in ballads as one of the distinguished, who fought
and bled for the country.  This disposition on
the part of Evered was very embarrassing to
Power; he had enough to do to resist the soli-
citations and expectations of those who used
every influence, coupled with intimidation, in
their power to induce him to leave his home.
Power wished Evered at home, at the bottom of
the sea, and everywhere else, a thousand times
in the course of this short and eventful period.
The Government had not yet put forth its power.
He knew he would be watched, and an absence
of a very short duration from his home, would be
his ruin.  Power conferred with Helen, a young

girl, and took her advice. She was strong where he was weak, and she corrected his judgment, warped by impulse and persuasion. She said,—

" This effort is beneath contempt, and eventually will be considered by the Government as a necessity for severity after the repudiation of their clemency."

Power saw this; but for Helen, it would have been veiled from his vision by excitement and infatuation. Helen became alarmed; her courage failed her, as she saw her brother in a very excited state, and feared from what her lover told her, that he would be kidnapped, and made a tool of, to serve the turn of the conspirators in any emergency that he could be useful to them, and that they would be more ready to sacrifice him than not, which intensified her anxiety. She also remembered that he was an Englishman.

Helen was aware that her brother was in no state of mind to receive advice,—that any remonstrance on her part would be unavailing, and possibly intensify the desire of his already too willing mind to turn traitor to his country, and make himself a name. Evered was almost literally held in leash by Power; he used his

unseen influence amongst his old friends for
them to dissuade Evered from joining the con-
spiracy, and to reject his offers; for already he
had mixed himself up with the busy groups, and
thrust in his opinion and advice unasked for.
The price demanded of Power was his accession
to the old cause for this protecting care over his
friend. The conspirators had now to betake
themselves to the mountains, and they had
again to resort to the use of spies for their
communications with the towns. The minstrel
was again busy, her harp was restrung, and she
was now used in delivering messages, supplica-
tions, and entreaties to Power. Power indulged
Helen, when she said "she should like to see
the minstrel, and speak to her as his own affi-
anced bride." The minstrel was allowed to speak
to her, and without her harp; that is, in her
natural character. Biddy was taken into confidence; and when the minstrel came on her
rounds, and stopped at Power's door, surrounded
with her usual audience, Biddy exercised her
prowess on the young spalpeens, and invited the
harpist inside the back door. She willingly accepted old Biddy's kindness, and ere long she
found herself in the breakfast-room with Mrs.

Power and her family group. Strange and restrained was the manner of the minstrel, but
she was not abashed; she had seen too much
and endured too much. She had the cause at
heart, and believed now fully that the hour of
Ireland's redemption had come, and the knell
of doom for England had struck. The accounts
of the magnitude of the expedition, and the state
of the North were not only contradictory, but
so exaggerated as to deceive none but those
who were blind; nevertheless, for the moment
some sober-minded and cautious people were
affected, and inclined to give expression to their
hitherto concealed hopes, whilst the rash and the
thoughtless were wild and ungovernable, causing
the whole of this part of the country to be in a
fever,—the plough to be laid aside, and the
pruning-hook turned into a spear. Full of this
feeling the minstrel encountered Power and his
family,—for to him, or for him she came. She
had known him before, and knew his disposition
well. Now she discovered a spell that bound
him, and believed in its potency when she saw
the sparkling countenance of Helen Trevernen,
heard her English voice, and felt the influence of her genial and winning manner. "I am

come for the master," she thought, "by intimidation, by pleading the love of country, by
ensuring success and rebuking him in forsaking
the cause, and losing the chance for glory; and
I may sing my wild songs in vain, for his ear is
deaf, my charm has ceased, and my spell is
broken!" Here was a charm she knew, as she
scanned the English maid, that she could not
break, and her heart forgot its cause for a moment in sympathy for Power, whom she greatly
respected, and in admiration for the girl of his
choice. She had allured Power before, and led
him captive by the strains from her harp and her
voice; but her masters, either too impulsive, or
too short-sighted, made a mistake in employing
her now. They had not calculated on an influence now brought to bear on their messenger,—
they never conceived the idea that she would
see Helen, much less be brought into contact
with her, in her persuasions with Power. The
old harp songs were to do duty again, but the
minstrel's hand had lost its cunning,—the harp
was left outside the breakfast-room, and she now
confronted Helen, and she silently pleaded for
Power. The minstrel had loved, unwisely and
too well,—her fount of sorrow had not dried

up, nor turned sour. Power had never wronged her,—had often been kind to her, and his mother was known the country over to have an open hand and a generous heart. She would like, if the cause prospered, to see Power at the head of his regiment, with banners flying and band playing, making his entry into Dublin; or, if the cause failed, to know that he is away from the trouble, with Helen at his side. Helen now spoke to her, and asked her "if she liked her"—she nearly said vagrant, but changed it into "troubadour life."

"Blessings on you for a dear, kind lady, ye need not have changed the word, sure it's a vagrant life!"

"But then why follow it?" said Helen. "There's Fred,—I mean Mr. Power."

"Call him Fred, darling, for I perceive he's your own entirely!"

Helen blushed before the twinkling and merry gaze of the singer. She was pleading for Power, woman with woman, but she was ignorant of it.

"I think," said Helen, "I have seen you before; there is something in your face and manner that is familiar."

"Troth, my lady," said the imperturbable

woman, "and where could your ladyship have seen such a vagrant?" laughingly emphasizing the word.

"For shame!" said Power, not knowing what disclosures she might choose to make in her fantastic mood.

"Be asy, now, or it's the song I'll be singing maybe far away without giving ye this bit of writing."

"Let's have it," said Power, hastily taking it.

"By my soul," she suddenly exclaimed, "it's the wrong one I have given! Ochone! ochone! what will I do?"

Whether this was intentionally done or not, neither Power nor Helen could discover. Power could hardly believe she made a mistake, and Helen marvelled at the conflict that she saw raging in her heaving breast.

"By my soul," she repeated, "ye should have had this one!" taking another letter from a concealed portion of her dress, and handing it to Power. Looking at Helen for a second, she then turned to Power, and said, "It's thrue, it's that warm-hearted girl that has saved you from following Emmett, and the like, to the gallows!" and, with a countenance calmed to rest,

she exclaimed, "May the Holy Vargin, and every
saint in Heaven bless ye both!" Then, with
earnest sympathy, she turned her looks on Helen,
and said with great meaning, "As ye have
crossed me in my mission, and stopped me from
persuading the master to join the patriots, I urge
ye to persuade him to flee from his island of sorrow!" With this she beamed a smile of the
utmost kindness on Helen and Power, and then
abruptly left the room. Whilst they were standing bewildered and amazed, she took her harp
from the outside and improvised the following
ballad, and warbled it in the garden-path beneath the window :—

" Ye heard the lark's song in the morning,
    As ye walked to the ould abbey door ;
Wild men in the mountain are scorning,
    They would lay you in death on its floor.

" Ye must leave this island of sorrow,
    Though dear as the home of your heart ;
Scarce wait for the dawn of to-morrow,
    From its shores for ever depart.

" There are those who will seek for your life,
    But flee like a bird through the air ;
Leave them to battle and strife,
    Their dangers you can never share.

" Then take the dear maid of your choice,
   In fealty she'll swear to obey ; ·
At the altar, there she'll rejoice,
   That from danger ye're hurried away.

" And safe o'er the sea may you sail,
   Escaped from danger and woe ;
Think a thought for the minstrel frail,
   Of kindness as homewards ye go.

" A home I never have known,
   A troubadour still must I be ;
Thanks for the kindliness shown,
   By Helen Trevernen to me.

" Farewell, be wedded and good,
   For trouble and sorrow are near ;
Soon we'll be deluged in blood,
   It's the doom of ould Ireland, dear."

Without waiting for any recognition, as soon as the fountain of her muse had run dry, she shouldered her harp and left, giving a trifle to ould Biddy as she called her, instead of receiving it.

As soon as she was gone Power left the room, followed by Helen.

" Dearest Fred," she said, " what dangers beset you now ? I fear for you, by your agitated countenance."

" Dearest Helen," he said, " I am in great
perplexity ; this woman has been diverted from
the object of her mission, and in a very extraordinary manner. I'll not read that letter to
you," he said, putting it aside ; " its contents
are enough to make me distracted ; but this one
I will read, and ask you what you think of it.
The letter," he said, " is from Merlin Tregarthen ;
he is now with his revenue cutter at the Cove of
Cork, where he arrived under very extraordinary
circumstances, by being chased by this squadron
which has caused the subsiding waters of rebellion to be more than ever disturbed again. The
letter you see, dearest, is addressed to me, but is
really intended for you and Evered. You were
puzzled just now, when this minstrel entwined
your name in her ballad, so was I ; I could not
then imagine her source of information, now it
is quite clear. She fell in with the sailors in the
course of her rounds, and twanged her harp, it
appears from the letter, to the delight of Merlin,
who rewarded her with a sailor's generosity, and
not without design, for, as he states, he has sent
his dispatch to the Admiral, and it is preposterous to suppose that this exhibition of force
can have any other effect than that of exaspera-

tion; therefore he anticipates that the dogs of war will be let loose with relentless fury as soon as the Government has breathed afresh, and taken their steps to punish this audacity. Merlin,—or the commander of the 'Sylvia' rather,—says all this, and insinuates more," said Power; "and if it is as he expects, he advises a precipitate retreat, and that without delay, to England on board his cutter before it is too late for him to render assistance, by our becoming suspects, and have then to flee for our lives."

"This is kind," said Helen, "and just what I should expect from Merlin. I do not know him, but we may thank Blanche for this, I am sure."

"Just as I may thank you," said Power, "for winning the minstrel, and charming her out of her wit and her seven senses. What say you, Helen?"

"Say!" said Helen, "to neglect this deliverance would be insane folly. Soon, very soon, the storm will break, and if Mr. Fred Power is in Ireland, he is not the man I take him for."

"But," said Power, "I am not inculpated."

" No, but you have been," said Helen; " it must be either Charybdis or Scylla with you, for, if you are protected by Government, you will be shot for a dead certainty."

" You seem to know our laws and customs," said Power.

" Alas, Fred, that I should say so; but it grieves me, and saddens me, to know that, amidst so much of heartiness and hospitality, there should be lurking everywhere, and for trivial reasons as well as the more fearful, the assassin's dagger!"

" It is too true," said Power; " it is a foul blot on my country. We will now consult mama," said Power, " for the urgent invitation includes all. It would appear," said Power to Helen on returning to the breakfast-room with the letter in his hand, " that the minstrel gave Merlin just the information he required. He knew you and Evered were in this neighbourhood, and, to his surprise and gratification, he found, in sounding the minstrel, that she knew all about us; so it was give and take with them; hence Helen Trevernen in the ballad."

Power was repeating this when he entered, and found his mother very sorrowful, for she saw

the coming storm, and felt the insecurity of life
and property to herself and son. The letter
which Power held in his hand, and now read,
had a magical effect on her; she embraced the
opportunity with eagerness, and held herself
ready at any time, so persuaded did she feel
that ere long there might be scenes of misery
enacted. There was one of the party, however, not at all disposed to acquiesce in these
arrangements. It was Evered; he received
the matter in altogether a different light.
"And as for Merlin" he said, "he would
drown them all. Damn him!—what's he doing
here?"

Helen now interposed, and exercised that influence over her brother which compelled him
to conduct himself with more propriety, and to
pay more attention to his manners.

Evered now had to follow in the throng, or be
left behind; he was not further consulted. Means
were taken by preconcerted arrangements to let
Merlin know that his invitation was gladly and
gratefully accepted; and at dead of night Biddy
was left in possession of Mrs. Power's house, in
charge of everything during her mistress's absence, so hurriedly was the departure made. At

night they travelled, and early in the morning
they found themselves visitors on board the
'Sylvia,' safe from the perils of an impending
insurrection, and under the tender care of Merlin
Tregarthen, who was awaiting to receive his final
missive from the Admiral, thanking him in the
name of the Government for his vigilance before
he sailed for home.

# CHAPTER II.

"Astounded, the reeling deck he paces,
  'Mid hurrying forms and ghastly faces."
                                    '*Isle of Palms.*'

THE last chapter concluded with the reception by
Merlin of his visitors on board his cutter, which
was quite ready to return to her station off the
Land's End. Mrs. Power and her party now
felt themselves secure and safe from danger.
All except one testified in their own way and
after their own fashion their sense of deliverance
from danger; that exception was Evered Trevernen, who had evinced throughout the same
unhappy and contradictory spirit. Merlin was
unaware of this; he remembered their last
meeting at Lamorna House, and hoped that now
his overture of friendship would be accepted as
he assiduously endeavoured to win his esteem by

every delicate attention at his command. Helen observed this, and was mortified when she saw these kindly and spontaneous advances, if not rudely, yet ill-naturedly repulsed. Power observed it also, and the effect it had on his warm nature was to open his heart to Merlin. Merlin felt it, and this contrast made the behaviour of Evered more reprehensible; there was palpably congeniality of temperament between Merlin and Power, as well as similitude in form, for both were fine men, which was apparent to Evered, and exacerbated his envious mind, and lashed it into an ungovernable fury which longed for opportunity to display itself.

Mrs. Power and Helen were provided with the best arrangements the ship could afford, and the two ladies were astonished at the ingenuity of the sailors in improvising for them so many comforts, as they knew very well there could be no preparations for ladies on board ships of this class. Helen was longing for an opportunity to become known to Merlin in her true character, but she had to restrain her enthusiasm, as Merlin had work to do. She had, however, occupation in arranging her cabin, and making the comforts placed at their disposal as advantageous as she

could.   Mrs. Power occupied her attention; she
was upset and exhausted from her unaccus-
tomed fatigue and excitement, and in Helen she
found a sweet consoler, as the merry-hearted girl
waited on her whilst she reposed on her sleeping
couch of rest, prepared for her in the Commander's
private cabin, which was appropriated for her and
Helen's special use.   Nor was she left to repose
only, for Helen fed her with dainties from the
generous hands of the sailors.

Such was Helen's occupation; she had, however, interstices of time to fill up, and she was
more than amused, she was interested, in looking
over a bachelor's domain.   She felt she was mistress here now, and inferred she had the privilege
of inspecting—she would not admit it was rum-
maging—the contents of the sanctum.   There
was much that she did not understand, such as a
spare barometer, compass, charts, and other sea-
faring gear, which was left, but placed aside;
there was the Commander's desk, unopened but
evidently not locked, yet as safe from the eye of
Helen's curiosity or scrutiny as if it had been
padlocked, although the Gipsy wondered whether
anything from Blanche was there, or had been
written thereon.   She suspected her fair cousin,

but experienced now a sensation of safety whilst arranging her cabin, and of gladness that she was about to return home; and overjoyed at her prospects, especially when she heard the manly voices of two men over her head, in conference together, solicitous for their comfort, and suggesting one with another little additional attentions for their amusement during the voyage.

Merlin's library was here, necessarily limited by space. Stepping up to the book case whilst Mrs. Power was taking a refreshing nap after her beef tea, she stood before it and paused, looking with her glistening eyes all over it. Taking the first book, on navigation, she said, "Know all men by these presents," and put it back; taking another which was 'Clarissa Harlowe,' she smiled and said "Humph! 'birds of a feather flock together.'" Looking inside the cover she read, " Merlin Tregarthen, cutter ' Sylvia,' from Blanche;" gently, without a smile, and without any' expression of surprise, she said, whisperingly, " Sacred to memory only," and at once replaced it. Still musing steadfastly before the book-case, her thoughts were, "Shall I intrude further?" and wistfully and smilingly, she allowed her hands still to play over the volumes, saying,

"Whene'er I take my walks abroad,
    How many books I see!"

She now handled one, it was Racine; Racine in
the original. "Shall I see the publisher's name
or the giver? Yes, ah! Blanche Laity,
Paris. Ah! Molière, my comédien. Yes!
Blanche Laity, Paris. Generous Blanche, how
she strives to relieve the tedium of midnight
hours at sea; why, she has parted with her
whole library," and turning away she repeated
the line already written,

"Whene'er I take my walks abroad,
    How many books I see!"

and slyly added,

"Whilst Blanche at home for books may starve,
    And I read hers merrily, merrily."

Merlin at length returned from the shore; he
advised his prisoners, as he called them, to keep
below as much as possible, and not attract notice.
This injunction was reluctantly obeyed by Power,
who was anxious to say good-bye to a few friends,
and leave some instructions, but this was inter-
dicted by one in command. Merlin's visit on

shore had two objects, one to receive his sailing orders, the other to load his gig with all the dainties and delicacies he could procure; having now satisfied his mind that his cook should have no excuse, he gave his orders for the hour of departure.

"My dear Merlin," Power said to him, as he ascended over the ship's side, "have you obliged me?"

"I have, Power," Merlin said.

It was a little matter of no consequence, only of considerate kindness, but it was now that the easy terms of friendship commenced. The outside barriers were broken down, the offer of manly friendship was made by Power, accepted and returned by Merlin, and seen by Helen Trevernen. "Where is Evered?" she thought; "why is he not included in this compact?"

He was there—she saw him bodily—smoking, with her great lustrous eyes, and heard his voice chatting with the boatswain, but she couldn't see him as she would have liked to have seen him; he had nothing in common with these men, nothing more than a barbarian, and she knew it and grieved for her brother, and became afraid of him; and now for the first time this element took possession of her as she saw him ripe for evil acts and dead to love. She thought of Blanche, and reasoned whether his love for her could have thus warped his ever wayward mind. She feared, that was her sensation now, that his temper had become soured by his Irish trip, and that he would be more unhappy than ever on his return.

The dinner hour had come, and there had been a promenade on the deck as an appetizer. Helen's last and enduring reflections were made at the time when she looked over the side of the ship, and saw the boat being rowed towards it, and the reception of the 'Sylvia's' commander by his crew.

Power would have chaperoned Helen below, but he yielded her in politeness to Merlin. Helen for the first time yielded to her generous impulses towards Merlin. She smiled, a twinkling wicked momentary smile on him, and accidentally touched his epaulette (Power had taught her strange tricks) and whispered "I wish Blanche was here." She gave no chance for reply; if her kindly manner didn't convey all she cloaked in her saying, the fault wasn't hers.

A happy party now sat down to dinner in the

'Sylvia's' cabin, including the commissioned officers of the ship. Merlin apologized for not having a minister on board. Helen in a moment glanced her eyes at him, full of wicked fun, and said, "You had one, I think, on board the 'Hercules,' or at least whilst you were at Malta."

Merlin understood her, and was equal to the occasion : he replied, "Frigates are entitled, by regulation, to ministers; it is only cutters who are blessed with divinities."

Mrs. Power laughed heartily, for she always relished the wit of Helen.

Evered now broke in; his attempt was not so happy, but welcomed as a return to good humour. He said, "I hope you won't cut away with them, but whether you do or not, let's cut away here."

Merlin half timid and apologetic, said, "Discipline and order are necessary to command, therefore I always, in the stead of a regular minister, say grace before meals."

Mrs. Power here said, "Happy and honoured are those who, subjected to such dangers as sailors are, can adopt such a course of conduct."

This made all clear for Merlin, and he rose modestly and asked a blessing.

Dinner was now served and he advised them

all to eat heartily, as he intimated that in a few hours in all probability they would be out at sea. The evening set in wet and windy, but the saloon or cabin of the cutter was well lighted up, and the fire burnt briskly, shedding a comfortable glare on the furniture, preventing Mrs. Power, Helen, and even Power and Evered from having any idea of the state of the weather.

Time passed swiftly, the cutter was at anchor, and well sheltered, therefore comparatively at rest. The ladies did not retire after dinner, but reclined on the one and only sofa in the cabin, whilst the gentlemen chatted over their wine, interrupted only by the warrant officer on duty coming and going with messages concerning the ship, when, and for a moment only, the wind was heard, and a very partial knowledge of the weather understood, so snug and comfortable was the cabin of the ' Sylvia,' and so agreeable the company. Tea was served with a continuous flow of conversation ; anticipations of home meetings and happy days to come were the subjects. Merlin had now to leave his cabin to attend to his ship ; the hour for weighing the anchor had arrived, and he examined his ship and gave forth his order to weigh. Very soon Mrs. Power and

Helen were made sensible of the delusion they had been under that the 'Sylvia's' cabin was a quiet place, and a sea voyage could not be so terrible a thing after all Merlin stepped below and told them he was now going to leave his moorings; he recommended the ladies to their couch, and appointed an urchin, or powder-monkey as he informed Mrs. Power, to attend upon them, which he feared might be necessary, unless they were very good sailors; this was put in as a little consolation, but it may be doubted whether the Commander did not exceed his strict warranty for truth. Mrs. Power feeling the vessel, as she described it to Helen and Power, more uneasy than before, had just conceived an idea that it might be rough, so she innocently asked Merlin if he thought it was so.

Poor Merlin; he knew it was rough, and that was a very sufficient reason for His Majesty's cutter to be at sea. He told Mrs. Power there was no danger in going to sea, and that there was plenty of wind, which would make the 'Sylvia' sail the faster; this satisfied the dear, kind-hearted lady. She was very glad there was plenty of wind, her conception of the term being analogous to plenty of corn for the poor, so that there may be

no complaining in the streets. Helen Trevernen
knew better, she was going home, and had therefore crossed the Channel before; besides, to use
her own significant term whilst in her cabin
fetching some trifling article for Mrs. Power, she
put her head out of window and was glad to draw
it back again, for her curls were blown to ribbons
and her hair was wet in a moment, by the rain
lashing against the glass. Helen now understood
what the powder-monkey was about when inter-
rogated by Mrs. Power when going into the
sanctum. "It was," as he told Helen, "to
make all fast, as they were going to have a
'sneezer!'"

Helen did not exactly apprehend the significance of the term in all its force when she
heard it, but she trembled a little lest she interpreted too correctly what the undiplomatic
powder-monkey had spoken. Helen ever after
that eventful night knew what a "sneezer" meant,
and often when the rain was pelting against her
windows at home, and the wind sent its fury in
gusts through the chimneys, would say, "There is
a sneezer to-night."

Helen imitated the powder-monkey, and did all
she could, in his language, to make all fast, by

going to her couch and covering herself with clothes, that is with shawls, which is quite orthodox with ladies who make all fast in sea travelling.

Power went on deck to see the anchor weighed, to hear the " Cheerily ho !" the " Heave ho !" of the men as they worked the windlass, and lifted the anchor from its bed. The 'Sylvia' in a moment felt her liberty, and was about to run wild like a captive Arab horse, but, if not with bit and bridle, she as perfectly felt the restraint from her helm, and like a good and obedient ship proceeded gracefully on her homeward course. Power well wrapped up in a monkey jacket and sea boots, looked wistfully over the ship's side and said adieu to the land of his birth. Like a true son of the soil, he gave vent to his feelings in rhyme, and with a cigar in his mouth he murmured his lament as the cutter was gathering way, yielding to the force of the wind as it was allowed to blow on the canvas, to carve a pathway through the wild watery waste at night.

> " Farewell to the land of my birth,
>     Farewell to the friends of my heart;
>   A fugitive over the earth,
>     From the home of my birth I depart.

" In exile I'll never forget,
    Thy scenes of beauty so rare ;
For years 'twill be memory yet,
    And regret I can never be there.

" A tear it falls from my eye,
    As the ship is leaving the land ;
My heart is relieved by the sigh
    That in vain I strive to withstand.

" In exile with many I go,
    To dwell on some kindlier shore ;
Free from the strife and the woe,
    The battles and warrings in store.

" I go with the hope in my breast,
    That happier times are at hand,
When passions are sleeping at rest,
    By ' the friends of my youth ' in the land."


(In sorrow this lament went into memory, from
thence it was scribbled on paper and appropriated by Helen, and by her kindness and permission is here transcribed to make more complete
this narrative.)

Power having gratified his feelings, felt the
uneasiness of the cutter, for she was now out to
sea, with a straight course right across the
Channel for the Land's End. He expressed
himself to Merlin, " that he felt the uneasiness

of the ship in his own uneasiness." Merlin told him "that they then must be both uneasy together, and advised him to turn in," which he did. Evered had done so for some time past, also in a very uneasy state, the only time he had been noticed, with all his eccentricities, in the condition of being overcome with drink.

As Power feared, and as Merlin expected, the night set in very stormy, so much so that all the hands forming the crew of the cutter were on duty. The powder-monkey boy had free ingress and egress to the ladies' cabin; he might have been an encumbrance and a nuisance in a drawing-room, with Dr. Fergus, but he was worth more than a thousand Doctor Fergus's now,— the boy was a genius in his way, for whilst he nursed Mrs. Power and Helen, he encouraged them, and even amused them with his atrocious falsehoods. He told them a score of times "they were making the land, and once round it," he informed them, "they would be in smooth water; that once in the English Channel, they would be as quiet as if they were in a mill-pond." He carried messages to Power, Evered, and Merlin; and brought them back from all except Evered, who was lucky or unlucky enough, in his circumstances, to sleep it out. Power was very ill, and very restless; he tried every conceivable posture, and every available specific against sea-sickness, but these believed-in amelioratives only mocked him, and aggravated his sufferings at every lurch of the cutter. Merlin appeared and vanished again and again, giving words of encouragement, and exhorting patience. When he was below in his transient visits, Helen always felt safer,—she could not account for it. Mrs. Power was exhausted, she had given up; life or death was alike to her, and was asleep. Helen became, as the night deepened, more wakeful. She now experienced the awful grandeur of the tempest, and the littleness of man when compared with it in any of his ways. "He had piled up Pelion," she said, "and removed mountains to some extent;" but here the plunging of the cutter was so violent, and her rolling so terrific, accompanied as it was with the blinding and instantaneous flashes of forked lightning, succeeded by Heaven's artillery thundering over the wild waste of waters, that in terror she fainted! Power was helpless, Evered was drunk, Mrs. Power neither dead nor alive, when the powder-monkey boy dashed some brandy-and-water in her face, which restored her senses; then, reeling and trembling, she accompanied the lurch of the cutter, and was precipitated into the cabin, but a few hours ago so snug and comfortable, and now a wet and dismal shelter only from the pitiless storm which was raging furiously. The lamp was burning but dimly, the water was over the cabin floor, forced in through the opened seams of the decks in the straining of the cutter. Helen shrieked with alarm; this brought Merlin to her side, though he could ill be spared. He lifted her light and fragile form in his arms, and was about to take her back into the sleeping cabin.

"Not there!—not there!—not there!" she said; "but on deck, Merlin! Oh, this awful night!"

At every time the companion door was opened floods of sea inundated the cabin, making it wretched, and it was therefore a matter of consequence to meddle with it now. Merlin could not stay here, his duty was on deck commanding. Unknown to Helen, he instantaneously decided what was best to be done; with a hurried command to the boy, who understood him, and was prompt to obey, he wrapped her in his pea-

jacket, and carried her in his arms in a half-
fainting condition on deck, which had ropes
placed here and there for the crew to hold on by.
Selecting a place in the middle, or waist of the
ship, Merlin deposited Helen, under the care of
the powder-monkey, lashed to the ropes, and
encased in tarpaulins, from whence she beheld
in horror the wild fury of the tempest, and saw
the nobility of manhood exquisitely displayed by
many seamen, but by none who were at all
comparable to Merlin. His reappearance gave
vigour and elasticity to the boatswain's orders.
Every man had his appointed duty; some were
pumping, this alarmed Helen, until reassured
that it was not a sign of danger, but a natural
necessity under these circumstances. When the
cutter was lifted on the huge waves, Helen was
frightened, but when she descended, she had
such a vivid impression of the language of the
Psalmist, "Thy waves and Thy billows are gone
over me," that she never forgot it. "It was,"
she said, "amidst the thunder and the lightning, and the wind howling through the rigging,
as if we were going down—down—down to destruction, for the eternal waves to roll over us!"
A shout was now passed along, "The bobstay is

broken!" and there was confusion by the displacement of men from their duties. Merlin passed before Helen; his countenance, she afterwards said, "I shall never forget; I can understand now what a hero may feel when he falls in battle; and oh, that I could delineate it on canvas!" The lives of all on board rested on the correctness or otherwise of his orders. The bobstay had to be replaced; on it depended the bowsprit, and on that the whole rigging. Calmly, he was in the midst of his men, deluged with sea as it swept along the cutter, and calmly and deliberately was the mischief repaired.

Hour after hour passed away,—endless to Helen as eternity was this night,—but *she* saw the first dawn of day in the glorious sun rising up and overtopping huge foam-crested waves, radiating a large space with brightness, spreading laterally and in altitude. Westward, over the seas, it was all blackness; cheerily did the crew work as the sun rose. Morning advanced, then Merlin passed, and said, "There's the land, Helen!" She knew it was right to look ahead, and she did, but saw nothing. The powder-monkey could, but then he had seen the land all through the night, and was not believed,—

Merlin was. Helen now looked, and saw something. "Depend upon it," she said, "that's it; what wonderful sight and intuition sailors must have!" Coffee was passed along, a cup invigorated Helen; she would not now be in the cabin for worlds,—her hopes rose, and her spirits with them. She knew the worst was over,—she felt well, that is comfortable, if she didn't move,—morning was come on, the land was now plainly visible; it appeared like heaven, in contrast to the gloom on her right as she reclined with her face towards the bows of the ship. The sailors enchanted her,—so noble in danger, and so kind, they couldn't help speaking to her,—it is said, "one touch of nature makes the whole world kin." It was so here; she had been one of them in storm, and shared their danger. One rough hand offered her, not rudely, a drink of coffee out of his can; it was accepted, the man touched his hat; she had done him an honour, helped his soul upwards, and ennobled him! Another, passing along fore and aft, said, "She must be a sailor's bride!"

Merlin had now more time at his command; the wind had moderated, and the waves were lulled, though they rose and fell angrily, almost lazily, as if they were tired, and had had enough of it for the present. The atmosphere was getting warm, and the ship quite comfortable; busy hands were busy swabbing and drying the deck, and coiling away ropes, whilst below what was going on Helen could not tell; she knew what it was like when she left it. Power at last, thoroughly ill, came on deck, and reposed by Helen's side, assisted there by Merlin with exquisite delicacy and manly friendship. Power was too ill to speak much. Merlin comforted him, and a sip of coffee revived him. Helen and Power were told that Mrs. Power had slept through it, and was now sitting up drinking her coffee, and listening to the powder-monkey, who had ingratiated himself and was a great favourite. The urchin never flinched throughout the night, but would have gone to the mast-head at the command of his master.

The cutter swept past the Long Ship's Lighthouse, and soon not only neared the Land but went round it, and was in the English Channel, proving to some small extent the truth of the assertion of the powder-monkey, that once there, they would be as still as if they were in a milk, possibly meaning a mill-pond. The set of the

tide favoured the near approach to land, and in
one of the many inlets, or little bays, protected
by bold headlands jutting out to sea, the cutter
glided into smooth water, and was sheltered from
wind and waves. The anchor was dropped, the
peculiar calling of the ' Sylvia' enabling her to
do effective duty under these conditions. The
cutter was now clean, dry, and lovely, and the
sails were drying in the sun breezes. Breakfast
on deck was preferred, and now Merlin brought
up Mrs. Power and placed her comfortably, when
she said, " The ship appears to be quite easy
now ;" and she remarked quickly, as she saw the
headlands, " that they reminded her of her island
home." She fancied they had had a very rough
passage, but she was very thankful she had
escaped a continuance of the suffering she was
exposed to at the outset. Evered was not in high
spirits ; he had a headache, a splitting one, but
he refreshed himself with brandy-and-soda, and
was ready for his breakfast.

At breakfast the party enjoyed themselves,
and warm friendships, begun in Cork, were now
cemented. They expected to be at Lamorna
House in the evening, and the day was resolving
itself into something after the fashion of a pic-

nic. Helen availed herself of an opportunity of expressing herself silently to Merlin, which he well understood.

"I shall never forget this night, and I shall talk with Blanche about it," she said.

"Do so," Merlin said laughingly.

Helen did not know that he was engaged; she did not know how Blanche had enjoyed his society, and had drunk the honey of his words, on board the 'Hercules,' under the spangled heavens; but she knew she had been protected by him in storm on board the 'Sylvia.' Perhaps, if Blanche knew of it, she might feel a pang of envy or jealousy,—most likely not, she would only be very, very sorry at Helen's alarm and inconvenience. Power now occupied her attention, when she pointed out to him the Logan Rock in the distance, and reminded him of the Balance Stone in Ireland. A visit to explore it was being agreed on, when Evered asked Merlin the size of it, and whether he thought half-a-dozen of his men could displace it. Merlin said, "he thought not, that it was easily rocked, it being so nicely balanced; but, beyond rocking it, he thought it would be difficult to displace it, especially so from its position, which presented obstacles for any leverage to be brought to bear upon it."

"What has seized Evered now?" said Helen. "I never saw such a face, it is lit up with mischief."

"Oh, nothing," said Power, "he does look like that sometimes, he used to after wine-parties at college; I expect he overdid it last night."

"Expect!—I know he did," Helen said.

Evered had turned away, for two ideas were here engendered on his brain, just on his arrival home after his friend's hospitality. The ruling passion was, as he could not be happy himself, and as he found he could not bear to see others so, he would contrive to make all miserable together. He knew that Helen had been on deck during the night, and had heard her express her admiration of Merlin. He would make Blanche jealous, and set her on Power; he would insinuate to Power that Helen had never forgotten Merlin since that night at sea, and that Blanche preferred him; he would spoil their little game of love-making, and ruin Master Merlin by persuading him and his crew of devils to upset the Logan Rock. Evered was in excellent spirits now, on his arrival; and his father, and especially his mother, rejoiced that the change of scene and the intimate friendship of Mr. Power had done him so much good.

The news of the arrival of the 'Sylvia,' with her returned voyagers, was dispatched to Lamorna House by a swift-footed messenger; and when the evening had set in, Mr. and Mrs. Trevernen were watching Mousehole Point from Lamorna House. Experience had taught Mr. Trevernen when the cutter might be expected, consequently they had no occasion to exercise patience, for at the period between evening and night, the cutter was seen coming round the Point, and making for the harbour of Pendeen. Promptly the party landed, and were received with warm welcomes and congratulations, leaving the 'Sylvia' at anchor in the bay, gracefully sitting on the undulating waters, undisturbed now by storm, under the moonbeams glistening over the expanse of the great and mighty deep.

Merlin was gratified; his reflections in his cabin, hallowed by its having been occupied by Helen Trevernen, with whom he desired to be friendly, were agreeable. He had made a friend in Power, and he felt now that his reception into society was secured. He sat down and wrote a love-letter to Blanche, the best thing he could do. Mrs. Power, Helen, and Evered were rest-ing, if not sleeping, after their fatigue. Not so Merlin ; he had now found opportunity for con-templation, as he recalled the strange incidents and results of his crossing and recrossing the Channel. He thought, with Blanche in fancy be-fore him, as he told her "that here had been Helen Trevernen, and of her heroic courage on deck in the storm ;" and wound up a long and loving letter by letting her know when he would be at the cottage. After this he slept, dog-tired, too worn-out to dream, but full of hope and love, as he became oblivious to life in deep and tranquil sleep. The trusty messenger had by no means finished his labour at Pendeen ; he very soon trotted off for St. Keverne and Tregarthen, where he delivered his dispatches. The news of the ' Sylvia's ' arrival was soon known at St. Keverne. The old bells rang out a peal ; well they might, for a little business, entirely satis-factory, had been accomplished during her ab-sence. Dr. Fergus was in ecstasies. Scrubby had an extra feed, and the demi-pique saddle was

cleaned, to be in readiness for a visit to Pendeen
in the morning. The Doctor had missed Helen
Trevernen more than he had any idea could be
possible; he had nobody to take off his fun,
and retaliate his cynical wit. He was, therefore,
impatient to see his fair combatant.

The dispatch from Merlin was duly received
at Tregarthen Hall, and the brief account of
the ' Sylvia's ' performance was the topic of the
evening's conversation between the father and
daughter, Sir Hugh suggesting that a kind letter
of congratulations be written at once to Pendeen,
and that he would go over himself and tell old
Kitty in the morning, as most likely Merlin
might be there. This made poor Blanche
tremble, for she wanted to go over in the morning, as she knew, but not her father, that Merlin
would be there. Blanche, for the only time in
her life, concocted a little plan, in which she
cajoled her father. She despised herself for her
dissimulation, and suffered in her own esteem;
but her letter from Merlin excited her, and made
her impatient. Such indiscretion as Blanche now
displayed, would have, under ordinary circumstances, caused suspicion to arise in her father's
mind; but it was not so, he was more excited,

and more impatient than his daughter to see
Merlin; and he thought of him only, for nature
was struggling hard to vindicate her violated
law in a father's suppressed love for his son.
Entanglement and mutual deception existed now
between father and daughter; fruit, bitter fruit,
springing up from erring ways. A great gloom-
cloud was now overhanging Tregarthen Hall,
when she said to her father "that she thought
it most likely Merlin would call at the Doctor's at St. Keverne, and that he and Merlin
would then come over to the Hall together, and
then Merlin would go home to the cottage to
see his grandmother, and spend the afternoon
and evening with her, unless invited to dine with
them."

Sir Hugh fell into the trap. He would wait
at home, and Blanche could drive over at once,
and tell old Kitty all the news, and tell her that
he should go over himself, perhaps walk over
in the evening with Merlin, as he wanted to
have a talk with him; and in the meantime he
remembered he had business to attend to, as
Mr. Marsh was coming, and this sent a cloud
over the forehead of the Baronet. He had been
worried of late; the Great Pendeen Consols Tin

Mine had been far more importunate in her demands than he at all contemplated, and he had
to permit Mr. Marsh to take out of the strong-
box in the muniment room more pieces of time-
honoured and valuable parchment, which were
very dusty, not having seen the light for many a
year.

Old Kitty was aware of the arrival of the
'Sylvia,' from little Beda, who had heard the
news at St. Keverne, where she had been on
errands ; and on her coming home she answered,
as usual, old Kitty's questions, and told her the
bells were ringing because the 'Sylvia' had come
back, for they all thought that she had been
taken by the squadron, or foundered.  She asked
Beda some more questions, and now became satisfied that the direct news had reached the Hall.

Blanche of late had been a frequent visitor at
the cottage, where she expressed her fears for
Merlin's safety ; so also had been Sir Hugh,
where he speculated, on his seat in the porch,
when wind and weather permitted, as to Merlin's chances of escape, and whether or not he
was now dead in his ship at the bottom of
the sea, having fought to the last, as he believed he would, rather than be captured and

allow his flag to be sullied. Well aware of
the 'Sylvia's' perilous position, he calculated
again and again Merlin's chances in detail to
old Kitty, and expressed his conviction that the
squadron seen off the land was another attempt
from France to corrupt Ireland and insult England,—but it would fail, of that he had no
doubt. Old Kitty remembering all this, saw
many difficulties in the coming to-morrow. She
expected Sir Hugh, as a matter of course. She
was sure Blanche would be over, to give Beda her
lesson, and she thought Merlin might arrive at
the same time; with this prospect of an inroad on
her peace on the morrow, Old Kitty took her
repose.

# CHAPTER III.

"Dost thou think, because thou art virtuous, there shall
be no more cakes and ale?"—'*Twelfth Night.*'

THE postman was punctual at the Hall in the
morning. Either the old man at the Lodge or
one of his children by deputy did this duty.
He was generally kidnapped, for there was a
diversity of interests at the Hall, and a multi-
plicity of correspondence. There were London
postdays, which brought the London newspapers
as well as letters. Mr. Bullock often disputed
the right of a first read with his master, and had
said to the housekeeper it was very reprehensible
on her part to retain it when she knew Sir Hugh
might ask for it at any moment; but this only
occurred occasionally, and when she was particularly interested in some celebrated trial.
When it did not contain any such harrowing

E 2

news as the last speech and confession of a mur-
derer, and his game at the gallows, Sir Hugh
was allowed to have first read, as Parliamentary
news, it was admitted, had not the same interest
for them. Bullock had defined ideas of truth
and untruth—his distinction was metaphysical—
he disliked the lie direct, it was vulgar, but the
evasion he revelled in. Sir Hugh had often
asked if the paper had come? This interroga-
tion required delicacy. "It had come, but no
further than the butler's pantry." "It had not
come," it had been brought; this was exquisite,
and after such diplomacy Mr. Bullock occasionally found his temper put out of joint on his
returning to his pantry and lifting the silver
dish-cover, and finding the paper, with the interesting and exciting account of the hanging
of some wretch, purloined by the housekeeper in
his absence while on duty at the breakfast-table.
It was, as he remarked to Mr. Marsh, "Mortify-
ing in the extreme."—"Highly reprehensible,"
would Mr. Marsh say, as he drank Mr. Bullock's
health. Sir Hugh had, however, once or twice,
either from suspicion or from some other motive,
demanded to know where the paper was. This
prevented all equivocation, and demanded from

Mr. Bullock the lie direct, which he abominated, and caused him to tell another tarradiddle by expressing his regret at having forgotten to bring it up.

"These are my afflictious," said Mr. Bullock, as he poured them out of his troubled heart into the sympathetic ear of Mr. Marsh, who washed them away with old Burgundy.

"Ah!" said Mr. Marsh, "the women give us a world of bother, Mr. Bullock."

"Indeed they do, Mr. Marsh. What do you think of that bottle?"

"Primo—*primissimo*," said Mr. Marsh.

"It is," said Mr. Bullock; "I haven't a finer bottle in the vaults."

"Why, it's twenty years old, Mr. Bullock."

"Twenty years!" exclaimed Mr. Bullock, "say fifty, and the finest vintage in the French records."

"It is fine," said Mr. Marsh, receiving from the gracious Bullock another bumper.

"No more," said Mr. Marsh; "I have business with the Baronet."

"True," said Mr. Bullock. "But now, Marsh," said Mr. Bullock. This was the only time he had presumed to dispense with the patronymic of

respect.  Mr. Marsh stared, and scowled.  Mr.
Bullock saw his error, and retreated.  He thought
him drunk enough at first to try his experiment
of equality.  He failed, and prudently corrected
himself by repetition, including the Mister as if
by accident omitted and not neglected.  This dis-
sipated the scowl of indignation from Mr. Marsh,
and gave Mr. Bullock the opportunity to talk
about Pendeen Consols.  Mr. Bullock had obtained his coveted share, and had paid his hundred
pounds of hard-earned savings, as he called it,
when drinking the choicest Burgundy, and was
getting anxious.  No one knew better than
Mr. Bullock the old proverb "that hope deferred
maketh the heart sick;" his hope had been now
deferred for some time, promises had not been
realized, and he wanted Mr. Marsh to take the
share off his hands and give him his hundred
pounds back by adding it to Sir Hugh's stake,—
as the addition would be so small, he would never
notice it.  The best Burgundy had been used as
an accessory, most confidential subjects on the
doings at the Hall had been told in the most
respectful manner, attempt at familiarity had
been tried, but all had failed.  Mr. Marsh
couldn't hear of such a plan as to add the share

to Sir Hugh's stake. He would try and sell it, but just now the thing couldn't be done; it would eventually be all right. Mr. Bullock groaned aloud; he had parted with his money, and now Sir Hugh's Burgundy only made him sad, whilst it made the merry Mr. Marsh exuberant, and patting poor Bullock on the back, he went out into the grounds, saying " Ta-ta," to prepare for Sir Hugh by walking off the effects of his Burgundy.

The newspaper this morning was left unread. Sir Hugh had his correspondence to attend to, and his preparations to make for his steward. Blanche had hers, but she had succeeded in her plans with her father, and was now buoyant in spirits and impatient for the hour when she would meet Merlin. She was exuberant, for a letter from Helen had caused her spirits to rise to a pitch of enthusiastic joy. Helen, with her power and tact, assumed as beyond disguise, that an understanding existed of a very tender character between her and Merlin, and succeeded in including in that assumption that she sympathized and expected to be trusted. All this she conveyed in a sentence or two, so that Blanche could not miss its significance, and having now

obtained her position, the remainder of her letter
was communicative and confidential. She told
Blanche of her own happiness in being engaged,
offered to narrate when they met how it came
about, and described with her peculiar vivacity
her delightful sensations when in Ireland, amidst
its scenery and her people. She longed to introduce her dear Blanche to Mrs. Power and to
Fred,—"her Fred." She told Blanche the circumstances—the "extraordinary circumstances"
she called them—which caused their coming
home in the 'Sylvia.' She bantered her in
detailing what she saw and what she did in
Merlin's cabin. She told her she must not be
angry with her when she praised her for her
bounteous generosity and forethought in render-
ing such assistance in relieving the tedium of
loneliness whilst at sea. "I admire the cabin
and the taste displayed there," she said. "But,
dear Blanche, the elegant little book-case so
well-fitted in the little nook prepared for it, with
its easy-chair in front, excited my admiration;
but when I surveyed the choice volumes, and
saw the name of Blanche Laity profusely scat-
tered over the pages, I was electrified, and
exclaimed, 'Bounteous cousin !' Believe me,

dearest cousin," she continued, "from what I personally experienced from the gentlemanly and kind manner of Merlin in storm, I cannot wonder that you should be more than prepossessed with his engaging and winning ways when you enjoyed his society in the beautiful summer evenings on board the 'Hercules' in the Mediterranean Sea. They must have been delightful, and easily account for every arrangement, or engagement, entered into, or about to be." With this letter in Blanche's hand, so courageously written and so evidently sincere, she stepped into her phaeton and drove off to give little Beda her lesson.

On her approaching the sign-post leading out from St. Keverne, just where she had to resist the addresses of her cousin Evered, she was startled out of her self-possession by observing a sailor gentleman walking up the hill towards the sign-post, just where she saw Jenkins when he appeared so opportunely in sight. She knew the form and step of the man in a moment. If the earth would open and swallow up her boy attendant for an hour or two it would be convenient, but that couldn't be; but to disarm suspicion was necessary. Blanche simply wanted to rush into the arms of Merlin and repose there, that was all! She wished she had walked, but she hadn't, and Dusty, her pony, was advancing fast. She felt the urchin's suspicions were awakened, and any manœuvre on her part would confirm them, and make him the hero of the Hall for that night. The moment was gone for any indecision; she restrained her feelings, and pulled up. "Mr. Tregarthen," she said, "how do you do? Papa is delighted to hear of your safe return. I am going over to give little Beda her lesson. I presume you are about going to the cottage; will you step into the phaeton and drive Dusty?"

Merlin, comprehending the pantomime, accepted her invitation, but declined driving Dusty; and turning to the urchin, said, "My lad, I am accustomed to rule the main, but I doubt if I could rule Dusty, as your mistress calls the pony."

The boy grinned. It wasn't exactly somehow as he expected,—folks did talk and boys did hear. He was puzzled, and if he spoke his sentiments they would have been to the effect "that, darney, Mistress Blanche ain't a-got no sweetheart arter all;" nevertheless, he had been taught to express himself with far more elegance when in the presence of his mistress since he had been taken from one of the farms and had followed Dusty to the Hall.

Nearing the cottage, Blanche gave the reins to her page, remarking they could walk the short distance that remained, and desiring Dusty to be driven home directly. Blanche then descended from her elegant phaeton, accompanied by Merlin, and they walked together to the cottage, not direct, but in a roundabout way which occupied more time and gave them full opportunity to post up all accounts that were in arrears and to plan for the future. They both talked of Helen Trevernen, Blanche showing her letter, and laughingly upbraiding him for his carelessness in allowing her eagle eye to scan the contents of his cabin. They both agreed she was very clever, and believed she was sincere, and were convinced of the impossibility of concealing their engagement from her, therefore Blanche gave Merlin to understand it was her intention to accept her overtures of confidence. Power was mentioned by Merlin, and in such a manner that Blanche was prepared for a very cordial introduction.

A short secluded path yet had to be trodden to bring the lovers from their circuitous walk to the cottage, and it was here that, walking amidst

the sunny hours of morning, the trying and de-
layed question was asked by Merlin when he
said, " Who am I, Blanche ?  Do you know ?"

This caused a blush to mantle over the countenance of Merlin, and a tear to fall from the
half-terrified Blanche, for she feared his pride was
going to make him rebel and forsake his love.  She
clung to him as it were, and fastened on him,
whilst she said, " I know not, but I conjecture,
Merlin."

" Blanche," Merlin said, with deep emotion,
" I have tried to get some information from Dr.
Fergus, and have failed, and again and again
from my grandmother, but in vain, and for anything I can learn I may have dropped from the
moon.  I have no relations, no friends, but who
are patrons."

" You have one, Merlin," Blanche said, " as
long as her pulse of life shall throb."

" Yes, dearest, but our engagement is concealed,
and were it known, what would your father say ?
And I cannot forget our first parting, when
reflection came, and you said, ' Oh, my father !' "

" Yes, Merlin, yes," said Blanche, " I remember that occasion well.  It was complete joy, and
yet complete sorrow."

"But who am I, Blanche? Can you tell me?"

"Would that I could, Merlin," she said, "and give you rest. I believe we are first cousins, but with the bar sinister that I will tell you, because I recollect Uncle Evered, after whom Cousin Evered Trevernen is named. I heard old Kitty say once he was at the christening at St. Keverne as Evered's godpapa, and Aunt Trevernen was doubtful about the baptismal water from St. Ruan; she suspected the good folks had forgotten it and had substituted other water, and that Evered would be unlucky. I faintly remember something of it; both of us were very, very young then. I remember also that Uncle Evered went away; and when he came home very ill and died, there was a grand funeral, and he wasn't buried in the old Laity tomb, but away near the old arch where the people were buried long centuries ago at Landewednack, and where the smugglers now hide their rundlets of brandy in their contraband and daring trade."

"Then you think, Blanche, that your Uncle Evered was my father, and somebody unknown was my mother, and he dying, I was taken care of by old Kitty Keskeys, and I took the name of Merlin Tregarthen?"

"I do, Merlin. I have asked old Kitty whether I am correct in my surmises, but she won't fully satisfy me. She says, 'One day,' and then, like you, I find all further efforts to obtain any information useless. I have tried persuasion to the utmost, for I am convinced she could enlighten us. But I hope, dear Merlin, in what I have told you that I have discovered the truth, and I also believe that one day you will be papa's heir, and I shall be your loving wife."

With this dream of imagination, which was satisfactory to Merlin, they found that time would not allow them further procrastination, and together they arrived at the porch, too late for Beda's lesson, but not too late to meet old Kitty's anger. She must have heard them coming, for she met them and prevented their entrance, and checked their expressions of kindness in the bud. She stood before them in her most forbidding aspect, both in dress and form; with one hand resting on her stick, and the other menacingly outstretched, she recited in her most dramatic manner the following malediction :—

"True as the needle to the pole,
　Which guides the seaman o'er the watery main,
Ye are come to read the fated scroll
　Of destiny that I must read aloud again.

Merlin, on a dark and dreary night
  On the wild and rockbound shore I stood ;
In vision then thou camest to sight,
  Thy face all marred with scars and blood.
The storm was at its height, and on its wave,
  Crested with foam, thy form was borne along ;
Cast up by storms, thy disturbed grave
  Yielding thee one from out the warrior throng.
The vision changed, and blanched with fear,
  Weeping was the girl that's trembling at thy side.
Down from her pallid cheek the tear
  Fell as she saw thee left by the receding tide ;
In shrouded mantle wrapt, she bent
  On the lifeless corpse upon the dreary beach,
Then seaward on the yeasty waves she went,
  Vanished from my gaze, and drifted out of reach."

"Blanche and Merlin," after a moment's pause she said, " what can this vision teach ?"

The lovers were disconcerted,—both were young, and not free from superstition. They intended to be very loving with old Kitty in the cottage, and thus obtain a tacit acquiescence on her part to their engagement. They were foiled and disappointed,—after this reception the cottage could not be a resort for their meetings ; if meet they will, it must be in the woods, for the old woman would have no part or lot in the matter. They thought her cruel, and Blanche expressed herself hurt at her unkindness, but old

Kitty had again played her part, and knew she had now given them such a warning as would she hoped help them to reflect. Old Kitty had not forgotten the days when she was young, and this effort tried her sorely.

Blanche gave a little attention to Beda for form's sake, and was surprised that the hour was so late,—time had flown with her. She had now to say "good-bye" to Merlin, and leave him with his grandmother.

Immediately Blanche left the cottage she perceived her father approaching, and hastened to meet him, and with an assumed manner she told him that Merlin was inside, that she had given little Beda her lesson, and that she thought he would have been there earlier, and they could have walked home together.

"And so we could, and so we will, Blanche; turn back with me. I should have been here before, but I have had to transact business with the steward." A dark cloud now overcast the countenance of the Baronet. "Do you know, Blanche," he said, "I am grieved that I am an adventurer in the Great Pendeen Consols Mine. I had no idea that I had so large a stake in it,—I find I am quite pinched for money. I hope there will be no more demands on me. I must see your Uncle Trevernen; I am quite disconcerted at finding to-day from Marsh that I am involved to such an extent. I did not understand your uncle after this fashion, Blanche."

Conveying this information to his daughter, he arrived at the porch, and saw Merlin and his grandmother from outside the window. Frank and hearty was the Baronet's reception of Merlin. He invited him to tell him in detail the incidents of his adventure, and said, 'Depend upon it, lad," —interrupting the narrative—"the Admiralty shall know my expectations. You shall have a frigate and the second epaulette,—and well he deserves it, Kitty," he said looking at her, and manifesting his undisguised admiration for Merlin. Blanche was bustling about in doubt and dread what old Kitty might believe it her duty to say now. She could say nothing,—she had exhausted herself, and she could not find it in her heart to sever them for ever by enlightening Sir Hugh. Merlin felt his position, and was very absent for one who was so disciplined by his professional education. The Baronet (it was the father speaking in him) forgave him, and was eager to make excuses for him. "Just come home,—the pleasure of seeing his grandmother and friends accounts for it all," thought Sir Hugh.

Hearing that Merlin intended being afloat again on the to-morrow, Sir Hugh would not let him off,—he must come home and dine with him at the Hall. He should be driven back. "And thus, Kitty," he said, "we will divide Merlin this time between us." This was a very satisfactory arrangement, and very soon father, daughter, and disguised son were walking together for Tregarthen Hall. The Baronet was very gracious and happy, walking between the two young people. What could they think of his extraordinary proceeding? Old Kitty could understand him, and perhaps ought to have instructed him, but she had procrastinated, and now she could not; but in reality he never thought of Blanche,—he thought only of making Merlin a gentleman, and one day taking him to his heart as his son.

The Baronet heard with pleasure as they walked along Merlin's description of Power, and he frightened both Blanche and Merlin out of their propriety when he turned to his daughter and said, "Why, he's just the man for you, Blanche!" Blanche coloured up, but did not reply. It was, however, a mere passing thought which occurred at the moment, and had no retention in his mind, and in a moment was gone for ever.

"At home at last!" was said as they walked up the magnificent avenue, crossed the spreading lawn, and were admitted into the beautiful Hall. They were seen coming by the household, and they in their turn were puzzled; some of them remembered Merlin a child, and had passed their information about him on to other and newer members of the kitchen, but here he was now a fine, handsome man, with the Baronet throwing his daughter at him. What could he mean? and if it was as some suspected, how foolish to act so!—he must be blind. Thus they thought and thus they talked, as from crevice and window the whole household stared at the party on arriving at the Hall. Mr. Bullock was master of himself, and was almost supercilious in his attention to the commander of the 'Sylvia.' Sir Hugh, however,—"to the manner native born,"—never looked so far down as to see what his servants thought of Merlin, his likeness to him, and the Laity family. The dinner was as usual, and Bullock was behind his master's chair, but his chagrin at not being able to comprehend

F 2

but a very small portion of the conversation, in consequence of its being in French, was very painful to him,—it prevented him from making a little social capital, and obtaining power and comforts from the kitchen below, and combating Mr. Marsh in importance. The dinner, however, in due time was finished without anything happening to further this narration. Merlin said good-bye, and was driven home to spend the last remnant of the evening and the night with his grandmother at the cottage.

# CHAPTER IV.

" The wandering mariner, whose eye explores
   The wealthiest isles, the most enchanting shores,
   Views not a realm so bountiful and fair,
   Nor breathes the spirit of a purer air."
                         JAMES MONTGOMERY: *Home.*

THE season of rest necessary after the stormy
voyage across the Channel having been enjoyed
by the travellers, they felt refreshed, and especially
Mrs. Power, who finding in Mrs. Trevernen a
lady of her own age, was animated with gratitude
and hope. Lamorna House was all bustle and
gaiety again with Helen's return to preside at
her tea-table, accompanied as she was by the gay
and handsome Irishman. The time for the
reception of visitors had come, and many friends
called with their hearty congratulations. Old
acquaintances were renewed by Power, and new

ones made by his mother. The carriage of Sir
Hugh Laity is now amongst the most conspicuous,
and hearty are the congratulations of both father
and daughter to the returned travellers, and
cordial the introduction to Mrs. Power and her
son,—more especially as Sir Hugh is informed
that General Power is leaving or has left India
for home, and that in consequence of the Irish
troubles probably he would be induced to make
his home in this neighbourhood, at least for a
time. This was very satisfactory to Sir Hugh
Laity, for he expressed himself to Mrs. Power
that he felt himself declining "into the sere and
yellow leaf," and that he felt himself becoming
less disposed to travel than ever, and more
dependent on the enjoyments of home and old
scenes with old faces for his consolations. Sir
Hugh took occasion to mention to Fred Power
his regret that he was not at home when he
visited Pendeen before, but now he hoped he
would see him often with the young people at
Tregarthen.

Having now paid his ceremonious call, and
given his invitation for a dinner party, he took
his leave, arranging to call for Blanche on his
way home in the evening after occupying the

day at the Institution, where he would meet Dr.
Fergus, busy as usual arranging forthcoming
lectures; and transacting business with Mr. Trevernen,—an occupation of necessity, he admitted,
but of horror and detestation, for he was getting
weary of the Great Pendeen Consols Mine, the
prospects of riches ever reminding him of the
passage in 'Macbeth' of keeping the promise to
the ear and breaking it to the hope when he was
called upon to supply fresh capital, which had
been very often of late, and to an extent far
beyond his intentions, as he always informed his
brother-in-law on these occasions. Sir Hugh
Laity had not become alarmed, but he had
become anxious at these incessant demands, and
he informed Mr. Trevernen, and even went as far
as to confess to him, that he had been obliged to
confer with Mr. Marsh, and had to allow certain
pieces of old dusty parchments, which had not
seen the light for many a day, to be deposited
as collateral security for accommodation at his
banker's, at which Mr. Trevernen appeared to be
surprised, but with which fact both he and his
son were perfectly familiar, and perhaps could
form an abler estimate of the extent than Sir
Hugh himself, and if they dared to look deep

enough down into their own hearts' convictions,
of the not improbable consequences also. They
knew that it was now become a necessity for the
mine to cut rich to save their credit, for other
speculative and unprofitable business had been
associated with the mine in which Sir Hugh was
unconsciously but legally involved, and the Tregarthen estate had become mortgaged to a far
larger extent than the grand old proprietor had
any conception of,—in a word, he had left these
things to Marsh, believing and trusting his
brother-in-law. His *carte blanche* had been
abused,—his name had been used as a power to
embark in transactions of a nature and to an extent
Mr. Trevernen would never have contemplated,
but that the temptation was too great to resist,—
the eager desire of becoming rich and great at
once, for at the hazard of the die, and the insidious
temptations of his son he had obscured his reason
and blunted the admonitions of conscience. True,
he sought consolation, and endeavoured to believe
he found it in the fact that these things were
tried for Sir Hugh's advantage, and if they
succeeded he would have had the benefit; but the
reasoning would not stand the crucial test in the
inner court, where no *nisi prius* reasoning is

allowed. He knew that his brother-in-law was ignorant of his position,—that he had virtually made him a sleeping partner, unknown to him, by taking a mean advantage of his ignorance of business in including him in these speculative transactions, which to his discomfort and alarm were turning out so adversely. Evered, too, had been drawing on him for money, but he was glad he was now at home to confer with; and he was now receiving great comfort from him by his assurances that "all will yet go well, and that if they lose on some of the transactions they will gain on others; and that although they must abandon all hope of profit, they need not contemplate or fear actual loss." "Evered," Mr. Trevernen resolved, "should go to London very soon, where he could get the earliest information to guide their judgment in these operations." This was comforting to a limited extent to the father, but his pillow was uneasy, and the sallies of Helen at her tea-table now she had come home again had lost their charm, and the gladness had gone out of his laugh when he heard them, which was noticed but not comprehended by the quick-eyed girl, as he answered at random, when the sad thought

floated across his brain that if these transactions
had or even yet could be successful they were in
fact for his benefit, and not Sir Hugh's. He
would have commission, brokerages, and part
profit, and Sir Hugh the lees,—yes, the lees;
and he knew it was so,—his inward monitor
would have it so, and no subtle reasoning of
Evered could cajole him out of the belief, and no
loving kindness of his wife, nor genial wit of
Helen at the social tea-table, could dispossess
him of this knowledge or make his heart glad,
and it was in this state of mind that he met Sir
Hugh and transacted business, and afterwards
returned home to tea.

Blanche and Helen availed themselves of the
earliest opportunity of a *tête-à-tête*. Their meeting now was affectionate and confidential,—they
understood each other. Old rivalries had done
their appointed work; they each had their orbit,
distinct as zones, wide as seas from each other,—
besides, both had found a pearl which each was
wearing in her heart of hearts. It was useless
for Blanche to attempt concealment,—Helen had
exhibited her pearl to Blanche, and proclaimed
its worth and beauty. Had she not done so,
there could have been no confidence between

the cousins,—it was this element of mutual trust that was breaking the ice of envy and jealousy, and which had kept them apart until now, whilst moreover it was Helen's sincerity as well as kindness to Blanche, now that she was in possession of her secret, that won her confidence and her love. Free from all embarrassment and affectation, Helen, as soon as she had Blanche alone, kissed her and told her " she was confident of her engagement with Merlin, and believed it to be but a natural consequence, for," said Helen, " I saw him in storm, saw him in danger,—and saw how he is beloved and trusted by his crew of bold and daring sailors. If I could admire him and almost love him in storm, what must you have felt in contemplative and meditative calm in the evenings on board the ' Hercules,' listening to his fascinating talk, so full of interest coming out of his own experiences!—for I assure you, Blanche, Merlin can talk; and if he talked on board the ' Hercules' under the starry heavens to you, who by constitution are just the character to drink your fill of love under these circumstances, as he talked to another certain damsel who shall be nameless (protected as she was by her avowed lover), but who nevertheless was certainly *hors*

*de combat* when he took her in his powerful arms
and carried her into the waist of the ship,—the
waist I think they call it, darling, but if I'm
wrong you can correct me, for your experience is
somewhat *en avant* of mine."

"Oh! Helen, Helen!" said Blanche.

"Dearest Blanche, I cannot help it," said the
laughing-eyed girl, as she continued, "yes, dearest, he took me by the waist (don't be jealous), I
was too ill and too frightened to say more than
that I was 'blanched' with fear; he understood
me, dearest, but to 'waste' no more words, if he
talked with that persuasive tongue of his to you,
for he appears to know how to avail himself of
opportunities, as he did to me, I should marvel
greatly if Cousin Blanche had not fallen deep
into the abyss of love, and remained insensible to
its delicious but tormenting sensations. Did
you," said the tormenting Helen, "like the
beautiful Desdemona in the play, see Merlin's
beauty in his mind, dear, and love him for the
dangers he had passed? It wouldn't have been
so with me, dear, I should have seen Merlin's
beauty whilst in his arms, but here comes Fred,
and we must have a little chat about 'ould Ireland,' as they call it, before we go out for our

constitutional; besides, I expect my Polyphemus here soon. I must present him to Power. The last time, we parted he was either full of Tam O'Shanter or whisky toddy. I believe, though, it was the former."

" Ken ye ever the like o' that, now?" said Dr. Fergus, who made his appearance at the moment and heard what Helen said.

" My dear Doctor, I'm delighted to see you," said Helen; " let me introduce you to Mr. Power. Mr. Power, Dr. Fergus."

" There's no occasion for that, ye silly guse," said the Doctor; " I ha' seen the lad before. I ken him weel. Ye brought him o'er to my cœnobitium a wile syne, and now I gather ye ha' wiled him o'er here a'together, but, lassie, let's see his mither," and forthwith the Doctor was introduced to Mrs. Power.

The Doctor was literally bursting with news; he had heard at the Institution that very morning from Sir Hugh Laity that General Power might be expected home at any time, and now there was an East Indiaman off in the bay, at anchor, just made the land, bound up Channel, landed her mails, and wanted supplies of vegetables and water. He informed Mrs. Power that he had

sent off a letter addressed to General Power, "informing him, my dear madam," he said, "of
your arrival here," and turning to her son, a
twinkling look of malicious fun, added "with
your turbulent and gallows-escaped son. Now
you see," he said, "if there is no General Power
on board, the letter will come back, but if there
should happen to be, we shall have the General
instead. In two hours, my dear madam," said
the Doctor, "we shall know our fate; meantime,"
taking the hand of Mrs. Power and feeling her
pulse, he implored her to be calm, that her pulse
was rising, but that he would take every possible
means to let her know the result without a
moment's delay; and with this as it appeared
quixotic, yet estimable trait in his character, he
hurried off to receive a man whom he had never
seen, and who was just as likely to be in India as
on board the anchored ship in the bay. He left
with the feeling that he should escort General
Power to Lamorna House in an hour or two, and
that his sagacity would have great commendation,
but this really had very little to do with the
Doctor's state of mind; he was restless as the
waves of the sea, always about other people's
affairs, known to every one, and known and be-

loved by everybody. The Doctor was seized with
an idea when he heard Sir Hugh Laity say in
the morning at the Institution that General
Power was expected home; before then he did
not know there was such a man. His only fault
was in communicating his idea and his operations
to Mrs. Power, but he had done so, and now he
was busy making inconceivable preparations for
the reception of a man who should have been a
friend of years, and whose arrival had been long
expected and was now announced. He had often
expressed his delight at new discoveries, and
was known to squander away his time in examining old curiosities of art, as well as consume his
time in revelling exuberance, by observing the
reign of law in the world of nature; but if now
his eccentric and wayward conduct should lead to
the landing of General Power, and cause him to
join his wife and son here, his gladness would
know no bounds. So thought the good folks at
Lamorna House, and so talked they as they
watched him walking down the street.

Very genial was the conversation between Fred
Power, Blanche, and Helen. Merlin was often
mentioned; and it was understood now, that a
clandestine engagement existed between Blanche

and Merlin, and some slight allusions were made,
as they walked through the town and returned
some visits, respecting the future and their prospects. Power was admitted into the secret;
perhaps Helen thought it discreet to have it so,
it might prevent awkward mistakes. Power must
be all her own; and thus they took their constitutional embosomed amidst the beautiful scenery
of the land, and gazing seaward on the rolling
ocean.

On their arrival home they found Mrs. Power
in hysterics, for the news had just been received
of the arrival of the General in the ' Chatanooga,'
strange as it may appear. The good Doctor
deeming it prudent to retain the General for a
short time on his landing, and send a messenger
to Mrs. Power to prepare her mind, "although,"
he said, "it was almost unnecessary, as I have
already done so, as I felt convinced the General
was on board."

General Power, somewhat of a martinet or
rather disciplinarian, was astonished at the display of freedom from Dr. Fergus, but the apparent kindness and interest shown atoned for it,
and was immediately forgotten in his joyous
prospects of so suddenly and strangely meeting

his family. Dr. Fergus soon made him aware of
the circumstances of their being here; that was
the finale of his day's work; and on their arrival
at the doorstep of Lamorna House, the General
had a clear perception of how matters stood, and
his pleasure was enhanced greatly in meeting
his beloved wife and son here, and not in troubled Ireland.

It is not necessary for the telling of this tale
to dwell on the happy meeting after so long an
absence, between General Power and his family;
suffice it to say, it was touching in the extreme,
beyond all doubt : but who could intrude into the
privacy of this meeting, or could be insensate
enough to look on and see the surcharged hearts,
discharging their happiness in tears?  None but
the frequenters of cock fights, and those whose
moral senses are blunted, and whose lives consist
in sensation, and too often, alas! in witnessing
animal torture, degrading though it be.

Yet there was one, a sparkling girl of wit, living
as it were on the border land, not yet inducted
into the family privileges; yet in the wilderness,
not yet in the promised land of holy matrimony,
who would like to have been there, and shared
in the scene of joy, and given out from her own

flooded nature welcomes and greetings. She had
seen the soldier unknown to him, had met his
eye, and like a guilty thing, affrighted, fled before it and hid herself in her own room. What
if he should disapprove of his son's choice! Had
she any fortune? had Fred the means of marrying? These thoughts for the first time rushed
through her brain and distracted her, and made
her tremble as she had never trembled before.

"I shall shrink within myself when I meet
him," she said.

But why should you, Helen? You are not wont
to act like this; you are bold enough with Dr.
Fergus, and repay his Rolands with your Olivers.

True, but so it is, anticipations affright us
more than realities. We dread the bark more
than we fear the bite; but with Helen it was now
her sensitive nature making her fear lest it might
be thought she had wooed, and had not been
won. Suspense to her was agony, but not for
ong was she left to self-torment.

Blanche soon retired and left her cousin; her
calm and sympathetic nature knew nothing of the
whirlwind that was splitting and rending asunder
the exquisitely sensitive and excitable system of
Helen. It was to her incomprehensible; she

saw it, because Helen was before her eyes quivering with agitation when she left her, but she
could not enter into the whirlwind and feel its
force. She could sorrow and grieve, had done
so often and often in solitude; but not now,
she would rejoice and wait patiently, reading to
beguile time until she was fetched, and then
would have met the General in conscious innocency
and expect as a matter of course his parental
salutation. Not so Helen. When Power fetched
her, her spirit was in convulsions, and but for tears,
she would have succumbed; but as an eagle is
not dazed by the sun, nor giddy in its altitude,
so Helen's spirit was made, so to speak, to live in
storm, to battle in it, to conquer in it, and to float
on the wings of the wind with delight; and so,
when once she met the gaze of the General she
was all herself,—Helen Trevernen with all her
idiosyncrasies. Enough, in hurried and confused
narrative, was soon told to General Power to
assure him that his son had made a wise choice
in Helen Trevernen; and his quick perceptions
instantaneously convinced him that such was ab-
solutely the case when he saw her enter the
room, leaning on the arm of Fred, his beloved
son. Helen approached the General as he stood

up to receive her, with true maiden modesty, not daring to look up, her countenance suffused with blushes; and not until she had the frank assurance of his approval of his son's engagement, did her dark and glistening eyes chase away her tears and flash out something of the energy of her soul.

"Oh, Sir," she said, timidly, looking up into the General's face, "it is Fred's fault;" but commingled with the look, there twinkled out from her eyes genial humour and sparkling fun. It had its effect; all restraint vanished in a moment, for the General took her to his arms, and kissing her, said, "I dare say it is, Helen. What say you to that, Fred?"

But before he could answer, the uncontrollable propensity of her impulsive nature broke forth, and, with a twinkling eye and furtive glance she said, "Oh, Sir, be sure he will say like his great ancestor, 'the woman beguiled me and I did eat.'"

This was her first flash of ready repartee, many in after days followed; intelligent glances passed from father to son, and Helen became one of the family.

The evening closed in with a large assemblage

at Lamorna House, where important subjects were arranged. General Power now met in the drawing-room Mr. and Mrs. Trevernen, Evered their son, Sir Hugh Laity and Blanche, and busy Dr. Fergus, who had in his eye, he said, a house and grounds exactly suited for the General, just a brisk half-hour's walk from here, and on the road to St. Keverne. He expatiated on its advantages with eloquent glee, which from any other character would be officious, if not offensive, but in the Doctor it was received as the most natural thing possible. He had arranged in his own mind that this residence would suit the Powers, and therefore it became his sole purpose for the time being to interest himself in the matter, to espouse the cause and get it done,—that was one of his terms, "get it done." And here he was recommending the residence to General Power before he knew his intentions, and before he had known him many hours, and on the very first evening of his extraordinary return; but he had displayed extraordinary sagacity, and had been the means of great rejoicing, and therefore he was privileged, but to General Power, who had been living in India for years, his eccentricity puzzled him, and his persuasion to remain perplexed him; but withal there was so much of heartiness, and so much that agreed with the General's inclinations, that his perplexities, like Rabelais' mile-stones, became further and further apart, until they disappeared altogether. And before the Doctor departed, it was understood that the General would go to London, and there transact his necessary business, and on his return would take up his abode at Pendeen, and that the Doctor should in the meantime go to work and secure the residence.

All formal ceremonies had now been completed, visits to Tregarthen Hall arranged, as well as to the Doctor's cœnobitium. The pall of night had fallen over the town of Pendeen, the carriage was at the door for Sir Hugh and Blanche, and 'Scrubby' for the Doctor, when after the kindest adieus, they departed for their respective homes.

# CHAPTER V.

"The unhappy salacacabia being removed, the places were filled with two pies, one of dormice liquored with syrup of white poppies, which the doctor had substituted in the room of toasted poppy seed, formerly eaten with honey for a dessert; and the other composed of a hock of pork baked in honey."—' *Peregrine Pickle.*'

A few days' rest at Lamorna House enabled General Power to realize his position, and to rest assured he was not dreaming on board the ' Chatanooga.' The sprightly disposition of Helen, and the satisfaction enjoyed by Mrs. Power at her sense of security and release from Irish anxiety, conjoined with her intense happiness in consequence of her husband's return, soon took effect on the General's mind, and convinced him that he was not dreaming, but living in the bosom of his family; but, nevertheless, under circumstances the most extraordinary.

It was necessary for him to report himself at head-quarters in London, but as the 'Chatanooga' had not as yet got further than Falmouth, being detained there by an easterly wind, he felt there was no occasion for him to hurry, and that he might remain with the kind friends he had so opportunely and strangely fallen in with, and in the meantime make many preliminary preparations for his permanently residing here, as he saw there were many inducements and many advantages in so doing.

At the breakfast table, before Mr. Trevernen left for his business, plans for the day were entered into, and the invitation of Sir Hugh Laity for a visit of some stay at Tregarthen Hall arranged, as well as a call on Dr. Fergus to express hearty thanks for his kindness, and reciprocate his overtures of friendship.

The day having arrived for visiting Tregarthen Hall, it was arranged that General Power and his party, including the Trevernens, should then pay a visit to Dr. Fergus at St. Keverne, and after spending the day there, the Trevernens should return to Lamorna House, and the Powers go on with Sir Hugh Laity to Tregarthen, who with Blanche were expected to meet the Powers at the Doctor's, and cement friendships by a grand meeting at the cœnobitium.

The weather was beautiful, and nature was adorned in her gayest and most seductive garments. The prospect over land and sea was entrancing, and peculiarly invigorating to the tried and climate-worn frame of the General, who expressed himself as being in a seventh heaven, so delicious and so restoring did he experience the balmy atmosphere, and the genial and sunny breezes playing over the grassy meads, and passing in shadows along the undulating and unbroken swell of ocean. St. Keverne's bells were sending their tuneful sounds along the road, and met the carriage with its happy party. "What are they ringing for?" was asked.

On arriving at the church tower, Helen solved the mystery; there was great merriment and excitement, mine host of the tavern was in his whitest apron, and wearing his gayest smile, there had been a wedding. Ned Jenkins, a nephew of Jenkins who had married Jenny Keskeys, was married to the saucy slut, Grace Runferman, and the men of the coves were just settling down at the 'Rose and Crown' to make a day and night of it.

Dr. Fergus's extraordinary house was within a stone's throw of the belfry, detached and built some twenty or thirty yards back from the main road, but connected with it by a large garden, thorn hedge, and a large gate painted white, on which was placed a copper plate, "Doctor Fergus;" but some one in a moment of waggish wickedness had by a little manipulation turned the letter F into P, which caused the plate to inform the locality that Dr. Pergus dwelt there, which to the curious would read very strange and sound very odd indeed if noticed. It had been in this state for some time. Merlin Tregarthen was generally believed to have been the delinquent in his boyhood days, but whether he was or not, he had the credit for it. At first the Doctor was very angry, although he laughed at the conceit, and inwardly relished the joke ; he gave peremptory orders for the plate to be taken down and sent into Pendeen to be restored, but it was, like many other orders of the Doctor's, if not disobeyed, certainly neglected or set aside, and so it remained until the eyes of the villagers became accustomed to it ; the joke grew old and was at last forgotten. The plate was cleaned weekly as usual, but such is habit, that the cleaner never

noticed what was on it. Whilst the plate was on
the gate, the Doctor would and did go in and out
a thousand times without noticing it, but take it
away, and he would miss something which gave
completeness to the horizon of his eye, and he
would then know that something was out of order
or out of place, and he would then by the law of
causation have remembered the joke that had
been played off upon him. But the plate remained, and the first thing Helen Trevernen saw
as the carriage approached, was the Doctor's extraordinary announcement, which caused the
sprightly Helen irresistible laughter and amusement; her flashing eye in a second conveying to
others in the carriage the reason of her cachin-
nation, they caught the infection, and the consequence was, the Doctor, who was in his garden and
walking towards his gate to receive his visitors,
was met with roars of laughter. Unconscious of
the reason, wondering what could have caused such
an ebullition of merriment, condemning Helen as
by instinct, and before any apologies could be
made, he cried out, " Are ye all daft ? but dinna ye
listen to the silly thing with her quillets o'
nonsense and scarts o' trash? But come in, lassie,"
he said, as he advanced to the steps of the car-

riage and handed Helen down, saying, "it's a sair confession I must e'en make, I can neither live with nor without ye."

Here Blanche now came up; she had been all the while looking over the Doctor's shoulder and listening to every word he said, and wondering what could have induced such excessive laughter from such a carriage full of demure people. The two cousins embraced each other affectionately and confidentially when "What is it, Helen?" was said by Blanche,

" Oh, don't ask, dear," she slily said; and with an askant look at the plate, she whispered, " It isn't Doctor Fergus professionally."

Sensitive and alive to the ridiculous in others, and ever on the watch, the acute ear of the Doctor caught the whisper, and in a moment he broke out, " Confound it, I forgot all about it; it was that boy Merlin, he did it, and I'll be revenged on him yet."

Blanche blushed when her lover's name was mentioned; there was magic in the word Merlin, and she trembled.

But Helen shielded her by saying, " Surely, Doctor, you don't mean to say that a trick has been played upon you?" (emphasizing the ' you '

as if it were an impossibility. " I believe it to be
your professional name ; your *nom de guerre* ;
your—"

"Na more! na more, hinny," he said with great
good humour.

All having alighted from the carriage, and
the cause of the laughter having been explained,
the Doctor welcomed them to his cœnobitium,
where they were joined by Sir Hugh Laity
himself.

The situation of the Doctor's dwelling in St.
Keverne church town has been described, not so
the cœnobitium itself, where he had long dwelt,
as it is generally termed, in single blessedness,
and where he occasionally entertained a few
gentlemen friends, and indulged in a rubber of
whist, old Parson Carnsew, as he was styled,
forming one of the cronies and the Baronet
another. Here he treasured up his curiosities,
and garnered up his erudite philosophic knowledge, and corresponded with the first *savans* of
the day; but hitherto his sanctum had been
avoided by his lady. friends as an abode where
horrible experiments were indulged in, and all
kinds of mysterious rites, after the fashion of the
renowned Doctor Faustus, were practised, but the ·

barrier had now been broken down and the
cœnobitium taken by assault.

There was much to astonish and surprise, if
not startle his fair visitors, and it took the
Doctor some little time to assure them that he
was not going to put on a magic robe and draw
a magic circle, and deal in the black art, as it was
called; but the genial spirit of the Doctor, as soon
as it had opportunity to display itself, soon dissi-
pated all such nonsensical fears, and his immense
acquirements soon interested his party, and
charmed their senses as he modestly and gradually
exposed and explained some of the wonders of
creation.

The house was peculiar; it was a large, old-
fashioned one, with a porch front and back, the
whole of the interior had been moved, leaving the
bare walls only; sleeping and cooking apartments
were adjuncts at the back, and communicated
with the one grand *salle* by the porch door.
There was a division across formed by a handsome curtain, like the drop scene in a theatre,
with this difference, instead of being one curtain
and lowered from the centre, it was in two meeting midway; when the division was required, it
was festooned up against each porch door, and

then the whole of the interior made one large lofty room. There were two entrances, a front and back, each one had two doors, or rather a door and a half, for the front or garden door of the porch was only about three feet high, and never locked; it served to keep out dogs, and to allow the poorer class of patients to enter at once into a vestibule where there were two seats, one on either side, and a mat for the feet; here they were sheltered from the rain or screened from the sun during the time that elapsed, and which occasionally was considerable, before the knock from a large brass knocker was answered from within by the Doctor himself or his attendant. One step down, when the knocker door was opened, and you were in the cœnobitium. Opposite the fireplace was his dispensing and surgical portion, where every bottle and instrument were beautifully clean and perfectly arranged; in continuation on one side, in cases with glass doors lined with silk attached to the wall, were bottles, etc. containing phenomena incidental to his profession, and on the other was his museum, where arranged in order he kept his minerals, shells, coins, and birds. In two large cases, facing each other, were his geological treasures, containing specimens collected with rare perseverance, of the flora from the carboniferous formations, and fossil organisms of the chalk; and in front or centre of this section was a large table on which were placed models of various inventions of the period : such was this division of the large saloon.

The other, that before the curtain, was furnished somewhat differently ; it was covered with a Turkey carpet and contained mahogany furniture of the best quality. On the walls were hung two or three valuable pictures, one by Vandervelde describing a sea fight, another by his contemporary Bachuysen, portraying the sea in calm, and one, a cabinet picture, portrait of himself by his friend Sir Joshua Reynolds, whom he had often met in London at the Bedford, in past years, with Johnson, Boswell, Goldsmith, Garrick, Sheridan, and others, composing the coterie of the celebrated men of his day. The remaining portion of the space was filled with little cases made expressly to fit every niche, and in which, catalogically arranged, was his extensive and well-formed library. One large easy-chair placed beside the fire, with a pair of slippers and a dressing-gown for winter evenings, with the velvet curtains drawn close, complete a description of the eccentric Doctor's dwelling, who was now in high feather, entertaining his friends, amongst whom was his "fair warrior," as he called her, Helen Trevernen.

The curtains were drawn concealing that portion of the room which contained his professional and scientific effects; but in front was laid on a large table a substantial lunch, where the Doctor dispensed his hospitality to his large party, informing them that dinner would be ready at the hour of four, post meridian. The transitional or "subsist meal," as the Doctor called it, in reference to the term used by the miners for their bi-monthly pay, was an unceremonial one, and one of genial results, by causing the barriers of reserve to be broken down and conversation to flow in wit and epigram in an easy and unconstrained manner, though not at the expense of good taste and decorum. Of course the Doctor's home was criticized, and the ladies did not spare him, but declared him to be, by the peculiar characteristics of his home, a true and unadulterated misogynist, and condemned him to do penance in the parish stocks. Helen affected trepidation, not knowing she said, with a sly look at Blanche, "what

might be the results of their gracious host's *cuisine,*
what simples he had compounded, and what
animals he had destroyed, for she well knew out
of his rusty, musty folios he could extract methods
of confection after the ancients, which would
defy the gastronomics of any modern epicure;"
and "for our dinner, I suppose, we shall have
fricassees the most curious, and *ragoûts* the most
horrid;" but, nevertheless, the lunch was of the
simplest kind, and the serving of the cleanest and
the neatest.

After the repast the Doctor had his curtains
festooned, his *salle* exposed in all its fair and
large proportions, and availed himself of the opportunity to exhibit his curiosities. Time failed
him to do more than display the extent of his
stored-up knowledge, for there was not a mineral
or a metal in his cabinet, a fossil or a flora in his
collection, but that he did instantaneously, on
being questioned, and sometimes by two or three
together, become a living and talking encyclo-
pædia, endearing himself by his artless and
loving nature, though concealed by his cynical
affectation.

Blanche was a silent listener, receiving without
question, if not absorbing the Doctor's lucid ex-

planations, yet endeavouring to understand them,
but often guilty of a truant disposition, which
made her a dull scholar, for she would say, "Yes"
when she should have said "No," and "Dear me!
Doctor, I never heard that so beautifully explained
before," when but a few minutes since her in-
structor had exercised his utmost ingenuity to
prepare her mind to understand him, but he was
never wearied ; she was Blanche Laity, and
he would have gone on with endless patience
lovingly pouring out his treasures at her feet,
and never expecting from her any reciprocity.
It was not there, and he knew it, and therefore
he was never irritated ; he, however, occasionally
opened the eyes of her intellect, and interested
her in botanical lore, for she was acquainted with
his garden, the oddest, queerest spot in the
round world, for he had there what the gardens
of Tregarthen had not; but she was Blanche
Laity, in his eyes a commanding and elegant
woman, and, in the language of his dear Shakspeare, "fit to lie by an emperor's side, and command him tasks." The Doctor was no misogynist,
or if he were, a very odd one.

Helen Trevernen, on the other hand, was all
eyes and all questions, peering into this and re-

quiring an answer to that; never satisfied, always
doubting, with an intellect always hungry and
always absorbing.

"By my troth!" Dr. Fergus would say, "she
keeps me going."

Sometimes she would teaze him and ask
foolish questions, and make silly remarks beneath
her well-known powers; this would annoy him
and make him wild, sometimes she would turn
sullen, but, like Una, she had tamed her lion and
feared him not; then suddenly would she display
such a perception and knowledge of the subject
then under consideration, that his ill-temper
would dissolve itself away, and he would exclaim,
"She is the bonniest lass in Christendom."

Leaving the Doctor in ecstasies explaining his
treasures, the ladies quietly withdrew to his
garden, and if they were astonished at what met
their view within doors, they were amazed at
what they saw now. Mrs. Trevernen and Mrs.
Power expressed themselves as surprised. Helen
and Blanche said it was the "oddest, queerest
place they ever saw." "What is this?" and
"what is that?" were expressions floating about in
the air until the Doctor and his party issued out
from the porch, when he immediately commenced

chaperoning his lively party over his garden. It was not very large and it was facing the high-road, but concealed by a large and well-trimmed thorn hedge.

" What is this ?" said Helen.

" This ? this is my refrigerating pan for painless tooth extraction," said the Doctor; and then he said "that the toothache was a very prevalent ailment amongst the labouring aborigines, so he had invented a refrigerator in which he plunged the heads of his patients, and before the numbness had gone off, occasioned by the dip, the tooth was out without pain;" indeed, he assured Helen and Blanche that on the principle that extremes meet, it was almost a pleasurable sensation, and invited them to realize it for themselves.

Helen and Blanche did not appreciate the Doctor's kindness, and declined his invitation.

" Good gracious ! what's that ?" said Blanche.

" Ah ! where ?" in affright said the Doctor.

" Ah ! take care, that is my leech cave; be careful how you place your foot, or you may have one on your dress."

With this pleasant information both Blanche and Helen sprang back in alarm; they were then assured by the eccentric Doctor that he would not play off any tricks on them.

"These, you see, are my moths," he said, diverting the attention of his party; "great beauties many of them, which I keep in all kinds of stages. Ah, if you would exercise a little patience, I would show you some of my experiments. Ye ken, I take a moth and put it under a glass, I light a bit of punk and put it under also; the gentle flutterer is stupified, and I then dip a pin in oxalic acid and pierce it, then I have him for my microscope and my collection, or for my dissecting knife. Metamorphosis, my dear Sirs," he said, turning to the gentlemen, "is the great law of life, and I assure you time flies with me in the contemplation of this law as illustrated in the phenomena I see daily around me. I see you smiling, lassies, but let me read you a moral. Surrounding circumstances should be made subordinate to us, not the reverse, and we should make all things minister to us. I assure you, man is not a contemplative being only, but an active one. I've been reading Spinoza, Sir Hugh, lately, and I detest the theory of pantheism more and more; my individuality the ages through will never be lost; my body is not myself; it is a tabernacle exquisitely moulded from earth's materials—from phosphates, sulphates, silica, and the like,—I dwell in it for a while, and sometimes under painful and uneasy circumstances, having difficulty to provide for its numerous and incessant wants, and I have much grumbling and contentions with it at what I consider its unreasonable importunities and little meannesses; but with all that I nourish it, and make it as comfortable as I can for myself."

"Like the snail does his shell, Doctor moralizer," said Helen.

"Just so, lassie, for I know its longing tendencies to go back to its elements."

"Like Ariel in the 'Tempest,'" ventured Blanche.

"Well done, lass! I did na think that ye culd ha' delivered yersel sa weel; but mair, my ne'er-do-weels, I improve the occasion and store up all I can in myself—in the caverns of my soul, if I may so speak,—for I dinna ken how much occasion I may have to draw on memory in the far country I'm ganging to, especially if I mind to be sociable amang strangers; besides, hinny, I'm no sure things are so very strange ayont, after all; there may be great analogies between

the two worlds, so the more I ken here, the more
I shall be kenned there; do ye see; that's canny,
isn't it? Ye would hardly think, now, what
treasures I have in this little parterre, so I have
christened it, and what bits of insight I have had
at times into the wondrous ways of the great
Architect of the Universe,—glimpses within the
veil to see the machines at work.   One thing ever
impresses me with delight, and that is the provisions made for the joyous life of every sentient
creature, intensified the more minute they become,
until the whole life is consummated in one pulse
of sensuous pleasure, with a dewdrop for a world,
and an hour for existence, until exhaled by the
sun from the dewlap of the cow browsing in yonder
meadow.   Yes, there is a great exception in
man's career.   Ye are quite right, Sir Hugh, there
is no denying it; it is very perplexing, but I dare
aver it was not always thus, nor need have been.
Ye ha' read yer Bibles, or suld ha' done so,
lassies, and ye ken there was naething noxious
in Paradise.''

"No fleas, Doctor?" slily said Helen.

"Weel a weel, I suld say no, lass, naething of
the sort."

"But then you have told us," said Helen, "and

lectured at Pendeen Scientific Institute, on the great unbroken chain of compensation, and how everything, even the most noxious, has its use, say fleas to keep people clean, for example."

"I have said all this I frankly admit," said the Doctor, "but I read that the whole creation groaneth in travail, which saying must have a meaning; and when I travelled in South America and along the broad Amazon, I thought weel if this economy suld ever be modified, and it may be, so as to supersede the necessity of many operations I see going on around me,—a place within the tropics, and maybe some few others, will be perfect Paradises to live in, when the necessity for all noxious things is superseded, and human life is simplified, which might be done by the All Wise as easily as he turned water into wine, multiplied the staff of life, restored paralysed limbs, and gave life to the dead. That, oh, ah! weel that is an adder; he came down to sup on frogs that were fattening for my scalpel on the banks of my fish-pond there, and he paid for his burglary by being caught. The ants are breakfasting on him; when they have finished, I shall have his skeleton for comparative examination. Ye see here is the division of labour, they earn their breakfast and

I win my skeleton. Ants are a very peculiar family. The females come out and found new families, so ye see, hinnies, ye are to be like the ants, and leave your fathers and mothers and cleave to your ain husbands. There's a lesson for ye, lads and lassies, for the human family do not agree under one roof, but each individual moves off and sets up a home for himsel'."

The Doctor observing certain talismanic signs going on between Helen and Power, stopped with an apparent objurgation. "I ken," he said, "weel enough ye are laughing at me, but bide a wee, and ye shall have hames of your ain. These are glowworms; night is the time to see them, but it is the female that emits the phosphorescent light. They are snail eaters; now ye think they are disgusting, weel ye are all too apt to be taken with outside appearances, and become disgusted when ye discover your Proteus devouring snails. But ye wish to know something about moths and butterflies, beautiful things, careering in gladness over meadow and stream. I have many specimens, which I will show you in my collection after dinner, but whilst we are here I will show you some curious creatures. Soho! here you are."

" What frightful little creatures! What are they?" all the party exclaimed.

" Weel, they are ca'ed 'burying beetles;' they will dig a furrow or ditch almost underneath a dead bird or mouse, and will push him into his grave; and here is another curious animal, a fish without eyes. It came from the celebrated grotto of Maddalena at Adelsberg, near Traun in the Tyrol. I visited the grotto with some friends. It is a very wonderful place, and amongst its wonders are these little eyeless fishes, evidently intended to live in the recesses where there are no effects from the solar light and heat, and the probability is, that their natural residence is in an extensive, deep, subterranean lake, from which they are forced through the crevices occasionally by floods or other convulsions, into this grotto. It is a great curiosity and has caused many papers to be written, and many discussions in the many scientific societies of our day. But I see you are all weary; my flora I must exhibit another day. I have some rare specimens, gifts of friends from many places, but my little parterre is to me a very charming place. In it I learnt to know that so wonderful is the economy in the animal and vegetable world that naething is lost, naething

wasted, each atom becomes the means of support-
ing some form of life or is resolved into its primi-
tive elements, in all cases to be compounded
with other atoms into new forms, and so on, until time has run its course. What is that in my
fish-pond, did ye say? Well, it is to be a steam
vessel. I heard it demonstrated at a lecture the
other day that, if a pair of wheels were made to
go round by steam in a ship, she would not go
on, but just stay still, like an obstinate chiel; and
it was proved to be the case by illustrating the
action of a mill-wheel; it wad na gang on, and so
it was proven that the vessel would be just like
the mill-wheel. I ventured to argue the contrairie way, and telled them they were talking
arrant nonsense, at which I was well laughed at,
and ca'ed behind my back an obstinate auld carle,
but I thought mysel', if the mill-wheel wad turn
the grindstones, it would send on the ship just as
weel, and that the mill-house had just naething
to do with the matter at all. I made the experiment just in the rough, and the little boatie
ganged along bonny. Vera soon I'll have my
experiments completed, and then the tables will
be turned I trow. I tell you, gentlemen, it's
mine own opinion that the time will come that

ships will go to America with wheels instead of sails, and folks to London on iron rails. Steam is a wonderful power, and we shall see great revolutions, mark my words."

" Oh Doctor! Doctor!" exclaimed the whole party, believing that his mind was in a state verging on hallucination.

" Weel weel! we'll say no more about it ; and now having seen my domain, we'll take a little turn down to the Coves and have a fling at the fish folk and then up to dinner."

Having spent an amusing hour in the Doctor's garden, the whole party walked up to the old church town, and admired the old ivy tower, with its goal for the hurling-ball, and looked at the sacred memorials of those who had played their part in their day, pretty much as they were now playing theirs, and deciphered as well as they could the old Cornish family names, and the odd conceits engraven on the now moss-covered and half-rotten tombstones.

Merry was the church town, and gay and noisy with the children playing their mimic game of hurling; many were the signs of respect from them, as they stopped their pursuit to look at the party so gaily dressed, and so happy with the

Doctor, and very many were the signs of recognition from him as he caught one rosy-faced urchin by the ear, and asked after his father who was away at one of the mines, or walked hand-in-hand with a romping girl, who held the corner of her pinafore, or " saveall" as it was called, in her other hand up to her face to conceal her trepidation, or attract the notice of her fellows as her eyes glanced out pride and gladness when she saw she attracted the envy of her fellow-playmates at this distinction. The Doctor was known by all and to all, looked up to and consulted in all the village concerns, and no 'sooner had he relinquished his hold on the child than the men and women made their way up to him, although he was with company; the men who were idling observing the strangers, taking the opportunity of informing him that great preparations were making for the wrestling match, and hoped his honour would subscribe ; this was called 'throwing a sprat to catch a mackerel." One man was severely reprimanded at not being at work, and was told he was well enough now, and ordered off, at which rebuke he skulked away. The women were loud, some had to tell what progress their children were making, who were passing through their sicknesses incidental to childhood, others again wailed out their fears and doubts as they were asked, "Well, and how is little Grace, and how is the boy?" for the real truth of the matter was, the worthy Doctor had not been his rounds that morning.

As the company passed along, the loiterers in and around the 'Rose and Crown' passed their remarks on the quality, and made their observations on the strangers as to who they were, whence they came, and what were they going to do. Fred Power was known, having been there before, and was recollected, and was judged to be the son of the elderly lady and gentleman who were now interesting themselves in visiting the old church and their worthy Doctor; such was their perspicacity, that they knew also that they were the party brought over from Ireland in the revenue cutter, and visiting the Trevernens at Lamorna House, but where the elderly gentleman came from puzzled them, and their curiosity was at fault, for they had not heard of the 'Chatanooga' having delivered up the General at the Doctor's request.

With kind words from Sir Hugh Laity as he acknowledged their warm-hearted and sincere

well-wishings, they passed on, leaving the beautiful village or church town behind them, and
facing the sea, descended over the downs, and
gradually wound their way down by a circuitous
path to the old fishing-cove, from whence they
walked along the seashore on this calm and
beautiful sunshiny day.    On their way down
they were met by several teams of horses and
bullocks, carting away the blue sand for manure,
with seaweed that had been torn up by late
storms, and dead fish which the fishermen had
been compelled to leave to decay, as the means,
in their day, at their command, were not sufficient
to get large catches away to the markets of the
country, where there were ample demands for the
commodity could it have been conveyed.

On the beach, drawn up high and dry, were the
fishing-boats waiting for the next tide at evening
to float them with their crews off to sea.    Their
owners or crews were idling away their leisure
time, some were sleeping on the sails underneath
their boats in shade, others were smoking their
pipes and had not finished drinking their ale in
wishing happiness to the newly married pair, the
parents of the bride and bridegroom being amongst
the number.    They had seen their children united

in matrimony, had heard old Parson Carnsew deliver precisely the same lecture on married duties and. obligations, and the necessity for temperance and frugality for happiness, as he had to them, and to all others belonging to the Coves and St. Keverne for the last fifty years. They had partaken of a good dinner, which was conspicuous for not having either fish or pasty, but a boiled leg of mutton and trimmings, with unquestionably a fair quantity of moonshine. This repast over and all ceremonies duly celebrated, their resources of amusement were exhausted; and time began to hang heavy on their hands, as the evening, the set time for the bout of drinking by the men at the 'Rose and Crown,' had not arrived and the interim had to be occupied; so following habit, here they were basking in the sun beneath their boats, and at the place where they spent the most bustling and exciting part of their lives in coming from and going to sea, and in landing the spoil from their nets. The children too were playing about, unconsciously receiving a preparation and education for the life of endurance and hardship which awaited most of them in the future: the elder boys were making and rigging little vessels, amusing themselves and delighting

the younger fry by sailing them in the ponds left
by the receding tide between the rocks, or even
on the great but now placid sea itself, which was
so lazy that it could hardly manage to coil over
its mantling wave on the beautifully curved and
resounding shore.   At times it was noticed by
Helen and Power, as they stood together on the
margin of the sea-line, that it was a question
whether the wave would coil or not; they saw
the gentle swell come undulating in until it
neared the shore, then it rose and paused as it
were for a second, then it inclined inwards and
fell languidly on the sand in one unbroken line,
with a plaintive moan-like sound, which was
continued onwards as far as the eye could reach,
along the circular sweep of water, until the turn
of the tide, when all would be changed by the
great income swell and roll of waters, filling up
the cavities and freshening the atmosphere of the
shore.

    "I hope you will like the fish I have taken up;
as I hear you are to have company to-day," said
one of the fish-wives to the Doctor.  "And I hope
you, Sir Hugh, will deal with the poor woman and
mother of a large family.   Haven't supplied the
Hall for the month; Mrs. Runferman has all the

custom now; she can't bring your honour finer or fresher mullet and pullock than I can, your honour, that she can't. Shall I take up the lot? they are all fresh, true as life, your honour, all brought in this morning. There's a lobster, Sir Hugh, for your salad, and there's a conger for steaks for your breakfast, better than any of them salmon that the Doctor tells us are caught in his country. I say, Sir Hugh, there is nothing better than your Scilly ling and Channel cod. Shall I take up the whole lot? There you shall have them cheap; I never drove a bargain with you in my life, though I have many with the Doctor, the huckstering, chaffering, skinflint, cut-me-down Scotchman, and be d—d to him. But will your honour take the lot? you shall have the whole for what you like, say a golden guinea, worth two, as I'm an honest woman."

"Worth how much?" bawled out the Doctor; "a guinea? you blethering auld sinner; they are not worth half the money; the mullets are small, and—and—"

"Well really, my good woman, I don't know," said Sir Hugh; "I leave these things to my people."

"Yes, your honour, and that you do, and pay

through the nose, and that's the way the slut
Grace Runferman got her finery and cockernonys
to catch young Jenkins. There, you shall have
the lot for half a guinea; really, your honour, it's
giving them away, why the Doctor there wouldn't
have the heart nor the courage to offer less."

"What, not the courage?" said the Doctor.
"Don't try me, that's all!"

"Really,—but here's Blanche," said Sir Hugh,
seeing her coming up, to his great relief; "speak
to her."

And she did, and told her story, how that Mrs.
Runferman had an unfair portion of the custom
of the Hall. Blanche promised that she would
speak to the housekeeper, and promised her for
the future a fair portion of the orders, and finally
pacified the eloquent pleading mother of a large
and increasing family by purchasing the lot of
fish at a guinea, which she declared was dirt
cheap, and the Doctor denounced as an imposi-
tion, and for which her legs ought to dangle in
the parish stocks. But the Doctor was not only
a privileged man, but his idiosyncrasies were
well understood; and having now pretty well for
the time said his say to the good fish-folks at the
cove, he joined his party, or rather they collected

themselves together and walked along the beach
in a compact little party, enjoying the scene, and
commenting freely on the sayings and doings of
the people who lived here in a little confined
world of their own. The tide had for some little
time ceased to ebb, and the more lively action of
the waves was noticed; the flood tide soon gave
the party to understand that it was necessary for
them to wend their way back, for the headlands
were so bold and extended seawards so far,
forming coves, or little bays, that they might be
caught between two of them if they incautiously
prolonged their stay; not that in fine weather, or
on a day like this, it would be of any consequence,
as the boats would put off from the cove and
bring them round the point, but in stormy weather
and in winter time the consequences would be
very serious, as poor Mrs. Power immediately
understood, and appreciating the difficulty in
imagination was for returning at once. This was
unnecessary, for although the tide was coming in
majestically, yet before it could come near to the
base of the headland, they would all be away and
probably at dinner.

In the distance, walking rapidly towards the
party from the cove, was seen a young man in

naval attire. "Who can that be?" said Sir Hugh
Laity. "It is like the step of Merlin, and just
his figure."

One amongst the party knew the step and the
form; he was unexpected, and she trembled and
looked at Helen Trevernen. "It is Merlin,
Papa," said Blanche. "You are quite right, and
I am glad your sight is so good as to distinguish
at such a distance."

"It is, Blanche, I'm thankful to say, about the
best organ I have left, for the gout, the arch-
enemy of man's understanding, has wellnigh
crippled my poor feet. Still I can do my constitutional; Doctor, that feat you will not deny
me?"

"That I will not," replied the Doctor, "and
I'm glad you are not effete yet."

"Oh, Doctor," said Mrs. Trevernen, "when
will you conquer your frightful habit?"

"Never, Mamma," broke in Helen, "it is his
taste and will stick to him through life, like it
does for cauld kail, sheep's trotters, parritch, and
haggis, all of which you will find he will give us
for dinner directly in some form or another. It
is sheep, sheep, all sheep!"

"Eh, lass, and I'll be vary mindfu' that ye

shall ha' your full share, for I'm of opinion that
ye would be a' the better for a little more of the
disposition of this useful animal, and a little less
of the chattering monkey!"

"You have it there, Helen," said Sir Hugh;
"but never mind, you'll get to windward of him
again, I dare be bound."

"That I shall, never fear, Uncle. He's playing
the lion now, but you'll see he has nothing but a
sheepskin to hide his recreant limbs."

"Quote correctly, lassie; it's a caulfskin."

"Oh, caulfskin, is it?" said Helen. "Can't
you speak English after all these years and say
calf? But there, there, you're too wise by
haulf,—I mean half," she said, tripping off and
away to meet Merlin, who had now joined the
party.

"Angels and ministers of grace defend us,"
said Sir Hugh, "and where did ye spring from,
lad? I'm glad to see you," and he held out his
hand affectionately.

"Merlin," said the Doctor, "knight of the
round table of old Tintagel, Crichton of my
heart! The earth has bubbles, as the water has,
have they cast thee up? But welcome, lad!"

"Hast eaten of the insane root?" said Helen,

turning to the Doctor; "then vanish into air and
melt as breath into the wind, and let me speak.
Merlin, son of the morning! welcome, thou who
hast trod the ooze of the salt deep and hast run
upon the sharp wind of the north!"

"Isn't it possible to understand in another
tongue? as Horatio says," stammered Power.
"But welcome, the graceful 'Sylvia's' worthy
commander!"

And thus was Merlin received by his friends,
and introduced to General Power most cordially
by Mrs. Power, who sang his praises for his
thoughtful kindness during their voyage from
Ireland. With lively *badinage* did the party, in
homely language, trudge homewards, and by the
tact of the devoted Helen did Merlin find himself
by the side of Blanche, and to the full did the
lovers enjoy after an absence of some time this
meeting, with the prospects of others, as Merlin's
stay on shore would be of some little duration, as
the 'Sylvia' was in port and careened to have
her copper sheathing examined and to undergo
· other repairs.

The party had barely come up to the cœnobitium, delighted with their walk and in the
highest spirits, when Mr. Trevernen and Evered

arrived in their carriage, just in time for dinner.
The Doctor's dinner party was now complete,
and punctually to the time fixed they sat down,
well disposed to do it justice.

"We are all very punctual, and thereby I'm
minded of a fine old Arab's saying," said the
Doctor, "that Englishmen build no minarets, for
they carry a muezzin in their breeches-pocket to
tell them when their dinner's ready."

"Then they are not like the Scotch, I suppose,"
said Helen, "for with them it isn't ' dinna forget,'
—beggarly set !"

After this, and the customary grace, mumbled
by old Parson Carnsew, the covers were removed,
and they partook of a plain but well-cooked
dinner, consisting of fish, joints, poultry, and
confections. To Helen Trevernen's apparent disappointment there were no *florentines, ragoûts,
soufflés,* and curious dishes for her to display her
wit and jests on. The truth was, the Doctor was
a very simple and abstemious man in his living,
and his disquisitions on cookery and recipes and
on odd dishes ended with his conversation.
Those rarities and conceits had no place outside
his imagination, they were Barmecide feasts.
True, he allowed the Trevernens by his talk at

their tea-table to suppose he indulged his appetite
and was an epicure, but his friends knew better,
and so might Helen, only she was so perverse.
The excellent plain dinner they now sat down to
was just what they all expected, but to the whole
party the dinner, beyond a necessary meal, was
of no importance, for they were all accustomed
to live on the daintiest fare.

# CHAPTER VI.

"No more with himself, or with nature at war,
 He thought as a sage, though he felt as a man."
                          JAMES BEATTIE: ' *The Hermit.*'

THERE had been a little episode, and it must now
be mentioned, which considerably ruffled for the
moment the Doctor's temper.  On his glancing
his eye over his well-spread table, he was pleased
with the arrangements of his domestics, headed
by old Jenny.  She was of Scotch pedigree, and
inherited all the freedom and testiness of old dependants, so characteristic of them in her day;
nor was she destitute of the shrewdness generally allowed to be bestowed on her country-
women, especially when the honour or dignity of
the family they serve is imperilled, by not only
adapting themselves to circumstances and taking
upon themselves responsibilities and cares un-

known to their masters and mistresses; but oft-times making shifts and deceptive appearances which involve them in difficulties, and make them ridiculous.

Old Jenny, unknown to the Doctor, had been to the Hall and made known her wants, and received all sufficient aid; and not contented with that, she had been to her old crony, Judith, at the Parson's, and had aid from her also. The table was well laid, and, to the Doctor's eagle eye, from his own resources; for he saw his old-fashioned decanters were on the table, also several solid silver cups, with the old family silver epergne for eight wax candles, beautifully cleaned up as a centre-piece. The borrowed articles, however, did not meet his eye, such as an extra dinner-service, and glasses, etc., from the Hall, and the surreptitious help of Judith's kitchen-maid. All was going well, smooth as a marriage-bell; his eye was complacent as he walked through the porch to his own dormitory to arrange his dress; that is, to don a little old-fashioned finery which very seldom saw daylight, in a frill to his shirt of point-lace, and a large diamond ring on his finger. *En route* he met Bullock, manifestly in working costume. With

an angry scowl the Doctor passed him without
notice, a most unusual act, and immediately
darted from the doorway an angry and terrified
glance into the kitchen, where he beheld, to his
mortification and amazement, in old Jenny's
treachery, his dishonour and downfall; for it was
full of auxiliary help from the Hall and the Parson's. Old Jenny was equal to the occasion,
she met the storm of wrath by bursting forth a
storm of words.

"Gang along wi' ye, what do ye here?
I'll pin a dishclout to your coat. Mind the
quality. For shame, peering into the kitchen,
as if ye begrudged the trimmings, and was mind
to look after the cheese-parings. It's no decent,
but ill-behaviour and ill-becoming." And slily
looking at her bewildered master, she said,
"What if they suld ken that you are here, and
not up decoring yoursel'? Gang awa, deary, and
the dinner shall do ye credit, or old Jenny will
dee. Here Susan! here Grace!" calling aloud
to her helps, and resuming her work. "Mind
the plates are a weel dusted, and het. Gang awa,
there; gang awa, there; I've not anither moment to spare." And heedless of her master's
intrusion, she continued bustling; and in a word,
as she said, "bustled him off."

The Doctor, let it be known, was a prudent
man, and knew the danger of carrying on a war
in an enemy's country.  He had rushed into it,
but now his choler had cooled down considerably;
possibly the fear of the dishclout might have exercised a salutary influence on him; and speechless, after a pause of a moment, he turned on
his heel, and departed from the shades below of
kitchen life, and ascended into the elysium of his
house, where he became a philosopher, laughed
at auld Jenny, resumed his wonted good temper,
resolved to let "naething" after this put him
out, and met his company like a gentleman.
Knowing that there was plenty of assistance, he
dismissed all care, and very soon found himself
very glad to be so much at his ease; indeed, he
improved the occasion by unconsciously, as it were,
letting his party know that he felt nothing of
the cares of housekeeping, having now, as was his
custom, left all arrangements to his people.  To
Helen and Blanche this little bye-play of the
Doctor's was productive of much amusement,
who knew his habits well, and who quizzed him
accordingly at his neglect of duties, and wondered how he managed so well, and whether he
had much trouble with his people, and whether

he found them at times inattentive. All this the
Doctor winced under, but like an able general, he
deployed, made a detour, and saved himself from
a complete rout from this artillery of Helen,
flanked by Blanche. Mrs. Trevernen was on
his right, Mrs. Power on the right of Sir Hugh
Laity, his *vis-à-vis*; the remainder sat promis-
cuously, excepting that Helen was next to Fred
Power, and Blanche between General Power and
Merlin. Very discursive was the conversation;
and perhaps a little less etiquette and reserve
than usual was observed under the circumstances
of a dinner at a bachelor's, and a supposed com-
pliment or necessity in consequence of being
less restrained, and therefore more noisy. The
dessert was very *recherché*, possibly Tregarthen
Hall may have supplied some of the dainties, but
if so, it was from old Jenny's whim and sensi-
tiveness, for the Doctor's own resources were all
that could be desired. Gradually the conversation, from being of a desultory nature, changed
its character, and formed itself into a discussion
on the acting of Garrick and his contemporaries,
and very animated it became, for all the elders
had seen the eminent actor. General Power had
seen him before he left for India, in his cele-

brated character of 'Abel Drugger;' it was in-
imitable, and he believed no man could ever play
it again, because another would never arise who
would have the characteristic qualifications. Sir
Hugh had seen him in Dryden's rehearsal, his character of 'Bayes;' the manager drilling his corps
and imitating contemporary actors, he considered
indescribably rich and humorous. The Doctor's
memory and experience not only covered a recollection of these celebrated performances, but
others; he had seen him play 'Harry Wildair,'
and fail comparatively after Peg Woffington's display of gaiety in it; but as ' Don Felix,' in the
" Wonder," and his round of Shakspearian characters of ' Lear,' ' Hamlet,' and 'Benedict,' he
said he treasured the recollections, and preserved
them in his memory as amongst the most exquisite privileges of his life's enjoyments. Dr.
Johnson's envy of Garrick, and the failure of his
play " Irene," were animadverted on ; and Dr.
Wilson, one of Garrick's admirers, who always
had a special seat in the pit when he played, was
allowed to have been by the Doctor, who knew
him, a very eccentric character.

" Boswell is a pedant," said the Doctor, "and
made himself so when all the world, for the mil-

lionth time went mad, and had a jubilee at
Stratford-on-Avon in honour of the Swan. I
was young then, and went to see the mummeries.
Foote was there, and little David, the life and
soul of it. I mind it well, there was speech-mak-
ing, and processions made up from the dresses
supplied from Old Drury, and plenty of rain, which
gave me a cold, and that's the way I retain such
a vivid recollection of it. What do I think of
Goldsmith or Goldy, as he is familiarly called?"
said the Doctor, as a beginning of his answer to
this question, "Well, I think he wrote like an
angel and talked like a fool, that's what I think
of him. I have often seen him, when I was
young, at the Bedford, and at Tim's Coffee-house
and the Doctor's club. But the place where he
was in high feather, was at the Literary Club,
founded in 1764. Little Davy said he would like
to be a member, and the surly bear, Dr. Johnson
(like little Davy, a Lichfield man), stamped his
foot with anger, and said it was presumption, that
he was not a literary man, and kept him out of it
for years. I may say I am an unworthy member
of this club, and I mourn the exit from its stage
of many loved friends. Look there, that portrait is by Sir Joshua Reynolds, a *souvenir*. I

highly prize it, more than my Vanderveldes, and almost as much as that little gem which I nearly lost the purchase of by being too hasty, a fault I'm not conscious of being troubled with."

"Indeed, Doctor," said Helen.

"Oh! oh, Doctor," said Blanche.

"Silence, ye catamarans," said the Doctor, amidst a peal of laughter; "I don't mean what you mean."

"Certainly not," insinuated the inexorable Helen; "you mean not too hasty to part with your money, eh, Doctor?"

"Weel, not exactly, lassie, though you are nearer the sense of my meaning; but I was about to say this little gem of Gerard Dow I had nearly lost by being too impatient, and bettering my offer too soon; but I secured it, neverthe-less, and learnt the lesson not to be over-hasty—"

"In believing the tales of beggars; eh, Doctor?" said Sir Hugh.

"Eh, just so."

"But to be more like Iago," broke in Helen; "never to wear your heart upon your sleeve, for daws to peck at."

The ladies now retired, the dessert was removed, coffee was served, and another hour swiftly passed away in examining the Doctor's folios, which contained engravings by Zoffany of Garrick in many of his celebrated characters; but, what was of much more value and interest, were some of Marc Antonio's fine engravings, and a couple of Rembrandt's etchings. The moon was now high in the heavens, the carriage for the Trevernens was at the door, and immediately they left for Lamorna House, leaving the Powers, with Helen, to accompany Blanche, in the Laity carriage, to pay their promised visit at Tregarthen Hall. As soon as the carriage drove off, it occurred to Blanche and Helen that as the moon was shining so beautifully, they would like a little walk on the seashore, and observe its effect on the sea. At this suggestion, so innocent, Sir Hugh Laity demurred, remarking that he thought they must all have had enough of the sea and the beach for the time. But at the repeated desire of Blanche, amounting to a solicitation of his permission, Sir Hugh immediately withdrew his opposition, out of affectionate deference to the wishes of his beloved daughter, and he now simply cautioned her against evening cold air, and recommended her not to forget her shawl, and not to extend her walk too far, or for too long a time. Blanche and Helen attired themselves for the occasion with great promptitude, and accepted the formal offers of Merlin Tregarthen and Fred Power to accompany them. Under these agreeable circumstances, they merrily tripped through the Doctor's garden, and hurriedly passed through the old church town, leaving the ' Rose and Crown,' with its dim glare and noisy drunken topers, to make a night of it in their own way, now the day had closed, and the evening had fairly set in, for them to enjoy themselves after their illegal manner, in consuming the raw spirit, or moonshine, as they called it. Gaily they tripped along, Blanche with Merlin, Helen with Power, indulging freely in lovers' privileges, and revelling in joyous gladness at this unforeseen opportunity.

These happy lovers embraced their brief hour, and enjoyed it, either by looking at the fickle moon, and making sonnets to her; or wafting melodious glee songs over the tranquil waste of waters, commingling with the mournful plash of the evening billow that resounded along the echoing shore, disturbing the night-screams of the garnet and petrel as they sailed along to their rocky home for the night; or when they looked on the fishing craft with their dim lights gliding gently away from cottage homes athwart the pathless deep in pursuit of their hardy and reckless calling, to earn the wherewithal to maintain the loved ones, young and old, in their humble cottages; or, as was most likely the case, discussing earnestly their prospects for the future. Simultaneously the Doctor, in his cœnobitium, had placed Mrs. Power very comfortably on his sofa, and proceeded to furnish his table with whisky-toddy, which he indulged in very moderately. The three gentlemen now closed up, as it is termed, and commenced discussing various subjects of interest until the young folks returned from their walk. All had travelled, and seen much of the world, and were men of experience, sagacity, and information. The various places that had been visited called forth their observations, and amongst others the Holy Land came to the surface. The Doctor was the only one who had visited Palestine, consequently he assumed rather a dictatorial manner in expressing himself on the many points that were opened out for conversation, as if the fact of his having been there gave him this advantage over his friends, and entitled him to the privilege of settling thereby every doubtful point in the conversation, and which was not always satisfactory to his listeners, for his views on many matters were, to say the least of it, peculiar to himself; but, irrespective of that, they were offensive to Sir Hugh because of the assumption of superiority of knowledge; therefore Sir Hugh, as was his misfortune, went into opposition on principle, and took up a line of argument opposed to his better reason; or, as the Doctor had said more than once before, on like occasions when he had exasperated him by his imperturbability, and rather mean advantage by demonstrating through his book lore the imperfect knowledge of his impulsive friend, that he argued against " the stomach of his sense." A delightful day was wellnigh spent, yet now the concluding hour had arrived, through the introduction of an old subject for discussion, it became apparent by the rising warmth of expression that it was probable that it would not close without ill-feeling engendered by this discussion, so unfortunately introduced.

" I tell ye, Sir Hugh," said the Doctor, " that you are altogether wrang in your history, in giving an antiquity greater to Jerusalem than to

Shechem. Lang before the covenanting people became a nation, old Father Abraham fixed his tent at Shechem when he had orders to get out of his ain country of Haran. There is a beginning for ye! Jacob, his grandson, bought th land of Hamor, and sank his celebrated well. That's possession! His ain little Joe, his beloved Rachel's son, lived here with them in their tent, and hither his bones were brought from the Nile. That's history! Here between two peaks, Ebal and Gerizim, Moses commanded the Law to be proclaimed afresh, clothing it with the terrific grandeur of Sinai,—and here Joshua called the tribes together, and demanded of them their free-will allegiance to Jehovah. And that's sacred history!"

"I grant all this," said Sir Hugh warmly; "and know it quite as well as if I had been on the spot; and can inform you that 'Shechem' was the capital of the ten tribes when they were led into captivity, but I aver the Jewish conquerors never annihilated the aborigines; and when they were led away, their places were filled by the multiplication of the old aborigines left behind: and although they adopted Jewish rites and ceremonies to some extent, yet I maintain again and again, Doctor, that the Samaritans in the Saviour's time were not Jews, because they were' not lineal descendants of Abraham, and had none of his blood in their veins. And, moreover, I read that Melchisedec met Abram at Salem—'the Jerusalem'—and ever after it was the Royal city; therefore from this fact, as well as its future history, I must be excused if I dissent from you in opinion, in giving priority of interest and antiquity to Shechem."

"I did na say interest," ejaculated the Doctor.

"Your string of stirring events flavoured very much of it," retorted Sir Hugh; "but whether you implied it or not, I maintain that such views as you have now favoured us with, in consequence of your visit to the Land, are preposterous and pedantic."

"Heard ye ever the like o' that now, General?" said the Doctor, gulping down his toddy to prevent an explosion of wrath at what he considered the obstinate and proud spirit of Sir Hugh refusing to be informed!

"And then, again," said Sir Hugh with warmth, "your strange notions about the tremendous consequences to the Jewish people, emanating out of the wars of the Maccabees, after their return from the Babylonish captivity. He has strange notions that everything was altered thereby, General,—that Moses was set aside for Judas Maccabeus, and that there was a great separation of the people into parties, and the construction of what he calls the ' Oral Law.' "

" So there was, decidedly," said the Doctor, " not a doubt of it !"

" And he says, General," continued Sir Hugh, " that the returned captives mourned after Babylon, like their ancestors did for the Egyptian fleshpots in the wilderness."

" So they did !" said the Doctor with extreme animation ; " not a shadow's doubt of it !"

" And that they," continued Sir Hugh with contempt and disdain in his manner, " regretted leaving, because Babylon was a beautiful city, and Judea and Jerusalem more or less a waste in consequence of the seventy years' captivity !"

" I tell ye, Sir Hugh," vociferated the Doctor, " it was so ! Babylon was, maybe, like London, full of what we may call civilized life ; Judea was just the contrairie ; and the people got to like the city style of life, that is, the fife and tabor in the taverns of the day, in preference to the pleugh of the villages of Palestine. And more," he said, addressing himself particularly to General Power, so as to convince him and get him on his side, "they forgot their ain mither tonguo, and took up with the orgies, or feasts as they ca'ed them, to the neglect of their own significant ones instituted by Moses; and they became, like an old wife's tale, forgotten and forsaken."

"How dare you say so, Doctor?" vehemently said Sir Hugh; "how can you express yourself so? What an aspersion upon the ancient people! Don't we know they hung their harps upon the willows when they remembered Zion, and were requested by their conquerors and taskmasters to sing them some of their exquisite chants, perhaps to amuse them in their *ennui*, or to mock their religion as they danced their disgusting dances to melodious minstrelsy?"

"That may have been," soothingly replied the Doctor, "and I doubt not it was so, for to some extent it is so recorded; but I maintain I am substantially correct in my assertions, and though I can't say they are confirmed by my own personal investigations, yet my inductive reasonings based upon information acquired by visiting the

locality of this deeply interesting history are assisted, and I am therefore led to form conclusions
different to those I otherwise should; and you
of all men, Sir Hugh, suld be the last to scoff or
contemn the information acquired by travel! Ye
have not been to the Holy Land!—weel I have;
and it wad be of little use my ganging there at
the cost of siller and the expense of strength, if I
did na carry awa' something in my ould noddle."
Being at fever-heat, the Doctor now exploded in
one long burst of declamation, which he intended
should settle this dispute for ever, and which
had been simmering in his mind for many a
day, and only wanted occasion to boil over.
After clearing his throat, and before his opponent could deprive him of his opportunity, he
said, " We must all admit that the fighting pro-
pensities of these Maccabee brothers were very
great, and that they knew how to make the most
of them. For they found their countrymen en-
slaved, but they left them free. That is one
great fact! When they fought, their faith was
obsolete, their temple was desecrated, reading
their law was prohibited, circumcision had
ceased, Sabbath observances forbidden on pain
of death, the succession of the high-priesthood

broken, the mother tongue out of date, Greek rising into vogue with the upper ten thousand, and Chaldee the popular language of the day."

The Doctor paused but for one moment to take breath, when Sir Hugh immediately broke in, and said, " I admit this to be a fair statement of the circumstances of the day," and was about to express his convictions, by saying that the Maccabees were the saviours of their country, when he was cut short by his exploding opponent, who thundered out,—

" Bide a wee—bide a wee, Sir Hugh! I say they were saviours, but to enslave it, and princes to abolish the Mosaic law and ritual."

"Nonsense!" broke in Sir Hugh with great warmth.

" I tell ye, Sir Hugh," said the now irritated controversialist with equal warmth, " that I can mak gude my assertion, for I aver that for thirteen hundred years of Hebrew history, no priest was made a king,—(but doubtless the first king paid dearly, when he made himsel' a priest, but this by the way),—I say the Maccabees overruled the auld custom, and set aside the line of Eleazar, and substituted their ainselves,— that's anither great fact! Then there was the

written law, to exist on and on without any
alteration. They set this aside,—that's ane
more fact to their discredit. Then again, there
was one faith, one service, one temple, one cove-
nant for all Israel; they trampled all this beneath their feet, and split the nation into sepa-
ratists, and created a code of law which was
encircled with mysterious rites! I say they
should not be exalted beyond their deserts; they
were fine fellows, I readily admit it, but had
they remembered Moses and ruled after his
fashion, they would have been much finer, and
have saved their countrymen from that condition they were found in when the angelic choir
announced to the shepherds in the illustrious
and historical town of Bethlehem, or Bread,—
where Rachel died when her husband, the
Sheikh, was on his way to Hebron, and where
Benoni, her child of sorrow named Benjamin, 'son
of my right hand,' was born; where the foreign
Moabitish lassie, Ruth, attracted the young
farmer, Boaz, and became his wife, and mother
to a line of kings; where her descendant, David, in the adjacent hills and Adullam caves,
slew his lion and his bear, and was anointed
king; and where in the fulness of time, vera

likely the identical home of Boaz and Ruth, the Virgin gave birth to her firstborn wondrous child, when the minstrelsy of heaven descended announcing in its strains, 'Peace on earth, and goodwill to man.'"

This peroration ran the Doctor ashore; he had delivered himself, and was supremely happy. Sir Hugh was silent, and he had succumbed, evidently. "But bide awee, Doctor!" Sir Hugh had indeed ceased to listen, but he had, as he considered, sustained his opinions, and, well satisfied with himself, left his opponent "to run himself out," as he had termed it on other occasions. For the last twenty minutes General Power and his lady had been neglected, so warm waxed the controversy between these two friends; and not being at all accustomed to their ways, they experienced great relief when they heard the young folks come bounding home, conscious though they were of having over-stayed the contemplated time, and rather ex-pecting a few words, at least of expostulation; but more than glad were they when they dis-covered that from some cause or another, time had passed swiftly away with Sir Hugh and the Doctor, and that they must have been interested, although a little alarm was evinced by Blanche when she noticed there was a great silence, which she interpreted "as a dead calm after a great storm." Sir Hugh and the Doctor had had their little differences before, and Blanche had been the mediatrix; fortunately now there was no occasion for Blanche's interference, as Sir Hugh said, "that he had enjoyed himself in pursuing an argument with his old friend in which he believed he had successfully maintained his position,"—and the Doctor said, "he had been delighted in discussing points of great interest in sacred history with his distinguished and esteemed friend Sir Hugh, whose perspicacity and extended information gave zest to the arguments involved; and, although they could not agree in opinion in all or many of the subjects discussed, because they did not see eye to eye alike,.yet he was weel pleased now as always to remember the old proverb, 'that differences of opinion suld never break down friendships.'"

"That is," said Helen, quoting another old saw, "old fads will always beat new ones in the long-run."

"Old fads," repeated the Doctor, "and where did ye get that from, lass? Query, *unde deri-*

*vatur!* I must use it in conversation with old Kitty next time, and see what she'll make of it. I must make a note of it," and, taking out his memorandum book, he did so.

It was now late, very late for St. Keverne life; old Parson Carnsew had been abed long ago. The carriage was ready, Merlin received an affectionate invitation to give the Hall as much of his time as his duty would permit whilst on shore, and with an order to jump in to be driven as far as the carriage would take him on his way to his grandmother's cottage, he did jump in, and somehow without any preparation, but naturally and as a matter of course took his seat beside Blanche, which was manifestly, to the newly-awakened eyes of her papa, allotted to him. Sir Hugh was about to say, "Why, Blanche!" but he did not; a new and a very strange thought took possession of his brain, which drove out the very recollection of his just having had another stiff argument with the Doctor. The splendid horses, fresh as daisies and impatient to get home, wheeled them rapidly along to the spot where Merlin alighted, and where Blanche met him in her pony-phaeton with 'Dusty' a short time ago. A kind good-night, and off

again spanked the brilliant team, and very soon
Sir Hugh and Blanche welcomed General Power
and his lady, their son, and Helen Trevernen, to
Tregarthen Hall.

And poor Merlin went along intoxicated with
pleasure, and yet murmuring at his lot in having
to go to his grandmother's lonely cottage for a
home whilst on land, after his enjoyments in
refined and accomplished society, as one of
them.

The Doctor had beaten his old adversary in
argument, at least he thought so,—had spent a
laborious but withal a very hilarious day,—above
all, he was very tired, so the pent-up and once
boiling wrath reserved for that old doitard Jenny
had grown cold; in a word, she was forgiven,
and on her sliding in to know if his honour
would like any more het water, and to say that
his nightcap was weel aired, and to know if he
wanted anything more, expecting now to feel the
fury of his anger, she was surprised, she was delighted to find that he wanted naething more,
and she was to pit his nightcap and gown just as
usual; "and eh, Jenny," said the weary Doctor,
"ye have had a bustling day, just tak a gude
glass o' whisky-toddy, 'twill circulate your bluid,

and mak ye sleep." With this Jenny retired, and the doors were bolted for the night. Fortunately neither the Doctor nor ' Scrubby' were wanted, and soon he was abed, snoring, being fast asleep!

# CHAPTER VII.

"Rosalind. O, how full of briers is this working-day world!

"Celia. They are but burs, cousin, thrown upon thee in holiday foolery: if we walk not in the trodden paths, our very petticoats will catch them."—'*As you Like it.*'

There was a great contrast between the occupants of the carriage that left the Doctor's for Lamorna House, and those in the carriage for Tregarthen Hall. Mr. Trevernen would rather have been spared his visit to his brother-in-law, but the party at the Doctor's was so numerous and hilarious, and his arrival so late, indeed, only just in time for dinner, that there had been no opportunity for the two brothers to talk business. Indeed, Mr. Trevernen studiously avoided any apparent likelihood in the conversation of Sir Hugh, or especially in that of the mercurial and unthinking Doctor, that might lead to inquiries

about Pendeen Consols Mine, although once or
twice it was manifest that such business thoughts
were pressing their way through the brains of
Sir Hugh, and opportunity alone was wanting
for them to have expression. When Mr. Trevernen left his mind was relieved, and he would
have been glad to have expressed his sense of
this relief to his son, Evered, as they were being
driven rapidly along, with Mrs. Trevernen sleeping, or concerned with her own thoughts, in
the corner of the carriage, and then by a confidential conference have received again such consolations from Evered as were becoming more
and more necessary for him to maintain his health
and his character. But in this expectation he
was disappointed, for his son was sullen, and
wretched in mind, for he had again endeavoured
to obliterate his sorrow, and drown his grief, in
stupor from excess of wine. What might have
been Evered's intentions when he arrived, perhaps he hardly knew himself, it is possible that he
still hoped to win his cousin's love; he did not
know of her engagement, or even her partiality for
Merlin, although when he allowed his reason to
exercise her judgment, he knew very well that
such must be the case. He did not know it

for a certainty, and hope whispered the delusive word " Persevere ;" but when he saw the party from the cove, including Merlin, all radiant with smiles and blooming with freshness, he knew very well that his hope was a delusion, and he abandoned it. He knew also that his sister Helen had espoused Merlin's cause, and he believed out of admiration for him, as well as love for Blanche, and then he hated her with an intensity of desperate hate. He had been tempted to make mischief by such pointed observations as to undeceive his uncle, as he perceived that he was kept in total ignorance of his daughter's predilections, and probable clandestine engagement, and so break up the party, and throw it into confusion. But he abstained, not from fear nor from kindness, but from hate, believing he could destroy the happiness and peace of his cousin and his sister more effectually by waiting a little, until his evil designs were more advanced. The temptation at the dinner was great; and it was a kind of satisfaction to him for the nonce to feel that in a moment he could turn their laughter into sorrow, and make them wretched. But he refrained, and took a glass of wine ; it was very good, he joined in the conversation, and took another glass. It was delicious, and gradually much wine drove out the devil of mischief, and he became like the man walking through dry places seeking rest, and finding none.   Evered was sitting opposite his father in the carriage, morose, sullen, dejected, and overpowered; and his father, having attempted conversation, fell back in despair, for he understood now the cause of his son's trouble and sorrow.   He saw the reason for the excess of drink; and beheld, to his horror, the stealthy and dark designs of his son, which he had by his avarice and ambition unconsciously fostered, and which he knew he had no power to frustrate. He might disapprove, but what of that; he knew he was in his son's power, and that he held him in contempt, for he had already tacitly acknowledged his connivance by the many sought-for occasions in which he had allowed his son to plaster over his conscience, and lull it asleep by his casuistry.   All he could say was, "Oh ! Evered, my son, my son," as he saw by the acts of his own hand, unless a miracle intervened, that ruinous consequences, involving Sir Hugh, as well as himself, must follow the engagements they had entered into.   At last they arrived at home and went to rest; if rest it can be called, to meet the to-morrows.

Merlin, too, arrived at his grandmother's cottage, dispirited, although he had spent such a happy day, and had been so joyously received on the sands by the whole party of his many friends. Yet there was a weight of sorrow abiding at his heart, and a cause for anxiety lest all his happiness might be as transient as a sunbeam. The one question, " Who am I ?" was still revolving in Merlin's mind, and what would be the consequences if Sir Hugh knew that he had dared to lift an eye of love towards his daughter, and what would be his act if he knew she had reciprocated his affection, and given her heart to an unknown man, or at least to one who had no ancestry, and who had been brought up in the cottage of a pensioned dependant ! Another thought harassed his noble spirit, " had he done right ?"—" was he still doing right in concealing his situation from Sir Hugh ?" " Was he quite sure, after all, that he did not know more than he dared to acknowledge,—that his obtuseness, if he were candid, was not assumed; and that he consoled himself that, after all, his grandmother was only playing a part, and preventing his engagement until some occasion would make it respectable by making it less unseemly to the world ?"

With thoughts of this character, Merlin arrived late at his grandmother's cottage, low-spirited, and his mind undergoing a kind of reaction, but indulging, nevertheless, in a little ill-temper. He had been highly favoured. Blanche had ever been as open as the day, but he had parted from her now without a kiss, and without that sensationalism so habitual with lovers in general, and with clandestine lovers in particular. There was no one last fond look, no spasmodic effort to tear away, no Romeotic whisper, " that parting is such sweet sorrow, that he could say good night until to-morrow." All was icy cold, cold as the pale moonbeams shining on them when they parted; no " Dear Merlin !" no " Blanche, idol of my heart !" nothing but a genial and a general good night, and a hearty " Come to the Hall, Merlin, as much as you can," from Sir Hugh, when the cattle again spanked off, and Merlin found himself precipitated from a carriage full of brilliant happiness, into the road silent and alone, with his thoughts only for his companions, and echoes from the woods for his answers. But at home he at last arrived; later, much later than old Kitty expected. She knew where he had been; and now whilst he was on shore, was

trembling with agitation. She could manage Sir
Hugh very well whilst Merlin was at sea. It
was her quiet time then; there was nothing doing,
only talk; and she could trim her discourse so as
to go with the stream, or stem the torrents of both
father and daughter as they respectively poured
their anxieties and hopes into her ears. But
now Merlin was on shore, her active troubles
would begin again, but not yet would she relin-
quish her old authority over him. And so, to
avoid conversation, and parry his questions—very
trying for her to answer,—she assumed the offensive, and demanded of him, " Why it was he was
so late," and affected to be weary, and a wanting
to be abed, although her aged frame was trembling with agitated delight, and the night long
would have been short for her to watch, so as to
hear again his voice, beloved to her, because she
knew by instinct that her furrowed cheek was dear
and beloved by him. Yet a feeble remnant of
desire to exercise control lingered in her mind, as
if to give it up was to snap a thread in the warp
that linked them; or may be, even yet, her habit,
inexorable, usurped its power, and she would
now, as of old, scold him as when he was a boy,
and came home late or wet, and irritated her.

So, receiving Merlin's embrace as customary of duty, affection, and respect, and scolding him too lovingly to leave any doubt for misapprehension on Merlin's mind, she forbade any conversation now, and directing him with her eye, he intuitively, in obedience to old habit, fetched down the old clasped bible, and laid it before her, snuffing the candles in the brass but well polished candlesticks, when he took his old childhood seat beside her, and listened reverently to her, when she, with design, which was well understood by Merlin, read portions for their evening exercise from the Holy Scriptures, appertaining to the life of David when a youth at Bethlehem, and where, under the direct providence of Jehovah, was, in the fulness of time, when disciplined and educated, brought forth from his shepherd's life, and anointed by him " a king." The exercise being over, Merlin retired to his own old sleeping apartment, and slept on a bed for cleanness that might rival the driven snow.

At the Hall on the following morning Sir Hugh met his company at breakfast, where really commenced his friendship with General Power; for until now they had only met in company, or

under circumstances which prevented the idiosyncrasies of character from finding expression,
and they could not know whether they would become fast friends by congeniality of sentiment.
But now, in the calm of his own house, Sir Hugh
could, in exercising his hospitality, discover the
bent of General Power's mind and disposition,
and either stimulate the feeling of friendship by
genial and confidential intercourse, or allow this
opportunity to pass away fruitless of such results.
Hitherto the stay at Pendeen of General Power
had been of a very unsettled nature, although
every accommodation had been resorted to, and
by Helen especially, to attach him to the locality ;
but he had not assimilated with Mr. Trevernen,
and both Helen and his son were aware that he
detested Evered, and that by Evered he was
held in aversion. The reasons for this antago-
nism were real, though not apparent; for the
General's experience of men and their character
had taught him to look with suspicion on this
young man, and to maintain towards him a certain
reserve. Helen, irrespective of her attachment,
he liked ; her character was open, she was sincere, and he understood her. Time, therefore,
had not ameliorated his condition; friendships

had not been formed, and the longer he stopped
at Lamorna House, the more uncomfortable he
felt. But now he felt, when sitting with Sir
Hugh at his breakfast-table, a freedom and happiness he had not experienced since his landing from the 'Chatanooga.' True, he was placed
in a position now highly conducive to produce
such a state of mind and repose, for the breakfast-room at Tregarthen Hall looked out on a
green sward of large extent, bounded by an
avenue of trees of ancient growth. The morning
was balmy, the sun was rising higher and higher
in his altitude, shedding a glory on the magnificent and tranquil scenery around; the gentle
breeze was loaded with the perfume of the garden
flowers from the slopes immediately before the
glass-door, which was wide open, to allow the
whole room to be filled with their aroma, whilst
borne along upon its wings was the gentle murmur
of the fountains set to play to keep the atmosphere cool and at a specific temperature. Here
it was that the General found himself at home
with his wife, and here commenced the friendship which lasted unbroken between these two
kindred spirits until rudely destroyed. Mutual expressions of regard escaped from each of these two

congenial minds; and after prolonging the ma-
tutinal meal to an unusual length, it was arranged
between them that after Sir Hugh had transacted
the necessary business of the day, during which
the General could read the London paper, and
dispatch his London correspondence, they would
walk together and enjoy the fine weather, whilst
the younger folks could take their ride. The
breakfast being over, the company separated.
Sir Hugh retired to his library, the General remaining, and occupying with his wife and son
the room for their correspondence, while Blanche
and Helen disappeared to ensconce themselves in
a sanctuary yclept Blanche's boudoir.

Bullock made his appearance in the library and
announced that Mr. Marsh, the steward, was waiting below when he brought the correspondence,
newspapers, etc. On receiving answers to his
questions for instructions, he disappeared, and
Mr. Marsh entered. The entrance of the steward
now discomposed the Baronet. The time was
when he was welcomed with a smile, with " Well,
Marsh, what's the news ?" and many affectionate
inquiries after the well-doing of the tenantry,
but now much of this was changed. There had
been no dinner last Christmas, and no festivities,

which were so enjoyable to the tenantry, especially to their wives and daughters, which made
the Laity family for generations so popular and
so beloved. It had been the custom once a year,
generally on New Year's Day, for the tenantry
to be invited at the Hall, where Sir Hugh's ancestors entertained them according to the fashion
of the day. Sir Hugh, although he had modern-
ized and beautified the Hall, had not allowed
this old custom to fall into disuse, but under
more refined circumstances had continued it.
The tenantry with their families assembled about
midday, and at one o'clock precisely they dined
in the great Hall. On the first and only gathering since Blanche had become mistress at the
Hall, a few friends were invited to assist her in
her new position. Sir Hugh on this occasion
adhered to old custom, and provided a plain but
sumptuous dinner of roast beef and plum-pud-
ing, with punch, the county drink. Sir Hugh,
as usual, made a speech, then his tenantry made
speeches also ; then the village choir performed,
and then the young farmers sang bucolic songs,
and then the quality retired. Immediately pipes
were introduced, and Mr. Marsh presided, and proposed more toasts, and encouraged more speech-

making from old and young, who by this time
were in a very genial condition, until the hour
when tea was served, when the Hall was cleared,
and the whole establishment joined in country
dances, reels, and finally Sir Roger de Coverley,
Sir Hugh selecting one of the elder dames of
the tenantry for his partner.

This custom had continued from generation to
generation, and was of a very endearing character, and was looked forward to with great
excitement. At times games had been introduced, but they languished for the want of support from the Hall; they were permitted, but not
encouraged, for Sir Hugh had no son who could
take the lead in them. But now there was an
element of rivalry which more than compensated
for any loss of interest from the want of games,
and that arose from the laudable endeavour of
the female portion of the tenantry to be selected
for the honour of dancing with Sir Hugh, or to
be specially invited by Blanche to accompany
her to the drawing-room, or by chance to her
boudoir, to assist her in any matter she might
have in hand. This feeling, however, was well
known to exist, and was well understood by Sir
Hugh, and he guarded against ill consequences by

avoiding invidious selections, and tutored Blanche
to be generous and free of her favours, but without undue selection.   The consequence was, as
it was known all could not dance with Sir Hugh,
there was more or less flutter with the matrons
as the evening advanced, and the time approached
for the one especial dance of the evening, as Sir
Hugh would good-humouredly excite his company,
and tickle their aspirations as a fisherman would a
trout.   More, Blanche, too, had a way of inviting
nearly all to her drawing-room in the course of
the evening.   She wanted so many little matters
arranged, that it was, " My dear Mrs. Tregony,
will you kindly help me here ?" and by taking her
into confidence to manage this little affair, she
made Mrs. Tregony a heaven to herself.  And "My
dear Miss Polsue, will you run to my boudoir,
you will find a scent-bottle, it is at the right-
hand side of my glove-box ?"   " Oh, Miss Harriot,
" I think you know where I keep my glove-box ;
will you kindly accompany your friend, and bring
the scent-bottle, white, with a gold stopper, and
be quick, Mrs. Penheath is far from well."   And
so these two laughing, blushing girls would run
and explore the boudoir ; and bounding back
with the scent-bottle, Blanche would go over to

Mrs. Penheath, and with a few laughing words, dash a quantity of the scent in the matron's pocket-handkerchief to refresh her; and anon, if her daughter Harriet was engaged, and her beau were present, the scent-bottle would ere long quietly find its way into Harriet's pocket, as a token of her regard, and an omen of good-luck. No wonder there was a little rivalry, and no wonder there was disappointment lest the good old custom would not be continued.

Mr. Marsh had come, and one part of his business was to tell the Baronet the tenantry's fears, and another was to solicit his patronage and support for the annual wrestling-match. These, after all, were minor matters of interest. The promise for the continuance of the gathering was given by Sir Hugh, for he said "He had no intention whatever to discontinue old customs, especially when they were so agreeable to his tenantry, and productive of such happy results." This point being settled, and the promise of the usual support, a pecuniary one, for the wrestling-match, all was right, and Mr. Marsh was enabled to announce that the annual dinner would take place at the Hall as usual, and with greater hospitality than ever, and that the subscription was

promised for the wrestling; which he did to the
tenantry, and public in general, so as to enhance
his popularity by his successful and clever diplomacy with the Baronet in their behalf.   But now
this being settled, another and far more serious
question of business was opened by Mr. Marsh.
More money was wanted, and boldly demanded,
as a necessity from which there was no escape, as
Sir Hugh had become liable for a large sum, in
consequence of the large share he had taken in
the " Great Pendeen Consols Mine."

Mr. Marsh, seeing Sir Hugh's consternation,
remarked to him,—he did admit with pain that
up to this period the mine had not answered expectations, but at the time when he embarked
there were such indications and assurances that
Mr. Trevernen was anxious that he should be
amply rewarded.   He had, he verily believed, from
the purest motive, allotted him a very large portion, even to the restriction and neglect of himself, and now almost with impudence, certainly
with boldness, he said, " The calls must be met."
Well knowing they must be, and without further parley, other old musty parchments from
the muniment room came forth, and Mr. Marsh
having now finished his business departed, and
left Sir Hugh bewildered and miserable.

The first thought was with Sir Hugh, "I will tell Blanche;" the second was, "I will go to London, accompany General Power; we will go together, and I will extricate myself at all costs from this business—this abominable business; what can I have been about? My steward even has the mastery over me, and Trevernen at the Doctor's table evaded and eluded every attempt I made to converse with him about business. I can never see him alone, that boy Evered is always with him, and appears to have his father under his thumb. I must rouse myself, and will! I will tell Blanche, and will see old Kitty, and that boy—oh, how I yearn after him, how handsome, how noble in bearing he is! How I would like to say, ' My son, Merlin, give me your arm.' I must confer with my son, but oh, woe is me! —woe is me! I have no heir, and I shall go down in sorrow to the grave!"

And so sat Sir Hugh in his elegant library, —surrounded with the beautiful, the elegant, and the ornate, and all that could be supposed to consummate earthly happiness,—wretched as he leaned his head in the hollow of his hand, on his library table covered with the best literature from his library shelves, and with the serials,

M 2

and journals, daily and hebdomadal, of his country.

Mr. Marsh, when he retired, was met by the obsequious butler, Mr. Bullock, and by him was provided with the best refreshment the Hall could produce.

"Well, what news, Mr. Marsh?" said Mr. Bullock.

"Well, humph, pretty well," said Mr. Marsh; "but my throat is a causeway of limestone, and I am as dry as a limekiln."

Here the butler bustled, and in his own scientific manner drew the cork from a bottle, and poured out a bumper of real Falernian wine, and handed it to Mr. Marsh in perfect silence. This worthy struggled hard with himself to detach one moment from the whole circle of time to gloat on the sparkling nectar, the unsurpassed quality of which he well comprehended, before he poured it like a river down his causeway, as he termed it, and, smacking his still thirsty lips without uttering a word, he extended the emptied glass towards Mr. Bullock, which he quickly filled again, not having removed from his position, well knowing what would be expected of him. This second glass having been emptied he remarked, "This *is* fine," and with little courtesy proceeded in a very cool and deliberate manner, in the language of the county, to fork the bottle, which, being translated into the vernacular, means emptying it. During this proceeding the obduracy of Mr. Marsh was more or less overcome, and he condescended to reply to Mr. Bullock's urgent inquiries, amounting to entreaties, after "Pendeen Consols," and what chance there was of his having his hard-earned savings, amounting to £100, back again? But Mr. Marsh only played with him, and tortured him; he gave him conditional promises, and no information that was of use; so poor Bullock had to hope on, and wait for better days; the old hope sustained him, he was in the same boat as Sir Hugh, and surely Mr. Trevernen would not deliberately ruin his brother-in-law. But then this hope would die out when he reflected on what he saw and what he heard when he went to St. Keverne church town, or to the fairs or to the market, but, above all, to the 'Rose and Crown' to have a glass and a chat of an evening, when they discussed there the prospects of Pendeen, and the management of Trevernen and Son. Mr. Marsh, having finished his

Falernian and his lunch, communicated the promise of a subscription for the wrestling, and took his leave for Pendeen to transact important business with Mr. Trevernen.

Blanche and Helen, it may be remembered, retired together from the breakfast to their sanctum. It is said that "fools rush in where angels fear to tread," and he would be a rash man, if not a fool, who would intrude into the sanctum of a lady, yclept a boudoir; nevertheless, in furtherance of the congruity of this tale, as far as this chapter is concerned, it is needful that for a brief while at least their sayings and doings should be chronicled. Together in Blanche's boudoir they were in earnest chat and conference; the Abigail had been dismissed, and with closed door and seated "en face" in a bow-window commanding a lovely view of forest, dell, glen, and dale, with a peep over the brow of a towering hill of the blue and distant sea, "a seat and scene," as Helen said to Blanche, "she supposed dear to her for fancy and imagination's sake."

"What fancies! What pictures has your fancy pictured here?" laughingly said Helen to the blushing Blanche. "How did you feel, dear,

when the wind was high, and alone you sat
here in solitude, listening to old Æolus,—that's
right, isn't it, Blanche? I suppose he has taught
you the sailors' names of the wind. I know a
little, very little; I know what is meant by 'a cap
full of wind;' but in winter, when the wind was
high, and you were sure the waves were rough,
and knew your Merlin was at sea, were you like
the ancient dames we read of, when their lords
were away to the Holy Land, sitting mute in
their ancient castles, and vowing vows of con-
stancy,—interceding with patron saints for the
success of their arms, and protection of their
noble selves, and waiting for their return? I
know not, fair Blanche, but I do believe you
pictured Merlin in his dainty cabin, fancied you
were by his side, and longed for his safe return,
and painted fancy pictures of happy meetings,
forgiving fathers, marrying Dr. Carnsews, and
giving away Dr. Ferguses."

" Oh, Helen, how you do prate !"

" Well, Blanche, it is my nature; and if I've
painted you, it is, after all, but myself had I been
similarly placed ; but, dear, you should have seen
Merlin as I have seen him in storm and in command."

" He is noble !" said Blanche.

" And generous as noble," said Helen.

And so they sat, and then Blanche talked of
Power, but her eloquence being of the more
silent class, she soon settled down to listen, and
Helen told her Irish tale, and her scene of love-
making, and described her walk with Power, and
how abruptly he asked her if she would be his
wife, and she said Yes, and the matter was settled ;
and then she bethought her of the Irish minstrel,
and told Blanche how interested she became in
her, and took from her pocket-book a packet of
letters and memoranda, and selected therefrom
a copy of the minstrel's minstrelsy, which she
read to Blanche. As the lovers were within the
sounds of their silver whistles, and they were
just now in that happy condition that Juliet
would like to have been with her Romeo
tethered to her—(" The woods are here," Helen
said in parenthesis, " for the echoes of our Romeo's names")—they had no occasion for letter-
writing; the source of solace to every lover ; so
in lieu of letters to Merlin and Fred, Blanche
made a copy of the minstrel's verses to Helen's
dictation. Thus whiled the happy morning
hour away, including sunny minutes reviewing

bonnets, dresses, wristlets of lace, and the last new fashion from Paris, until the moment for dressing for walk arrived, when, arm-in-arm, they walked up to the window and looked out on the magnificent scene, bounded by the broad acres of Blanche's father; and then it was with a loving kiss from Helen, warmly returned by Blanche, that the two cousins talked seriously.

Helen, in whispered confidence, said, "I have had my affairs settled, Blanche, and very trying they were; my courage was sadly put to the test when I met the General; but with you, Blanche dearest, nothing is settled, and therefore nothing is done. Have you thought seriously of your position, and have you considered all the consequences? Look out, dearest, on these broad acres,—remember your ancient lineage, think of your father and what he would do were he now to be informed of your engagement! Have you reflected on this matter sufficiently? And then, dearest, who is Merlin Tregarthen? People do say that he is the son of a poor woman, and has not the benefit of the Church's protection on his birth. I would not wound your feelings, dearest, but now we are together, and I am, through the accident chiefly of having been an intruder in

Merlin's cabin, the possessor of your secret, let me in affection urge you to consider deeply your position! I am persuaded you have committed your happiness to Merlin, and I would not be the one to urge you to an act of dishonour whereby you might imperil your own happiness as well as his. I have listened, dearest Blanche, to your story, and with intense interest to your descriptive interviews with old Kitty: she is very mysterious, and probably knows much more than she cares to reveal. I have listened attentively to your description of Sir Hugh's visits to her, and their conversations respecting Merlin, but I cannot gather anything from these two circumstances at all consolatory. If old Kitty, out of love to you and Merlin, had anything advantageous, she would not keep you in the dark, and discourage you so vehemently; depend upon it, cousin, what she knows is disastrous to your hopes, and she acts the spitfire not only to warn you of dangers you are but dimly conscious of, but to disenchant you, and save you from ruin. I do not know, dearest, who is the putative father of Merlin, it may be old Evered—"

"And if so," then eagerly said Blanche, "we are only cousins!"

" Only cousins !" echoed Helen ; and here the
conversation on this point suddenly and abruptly
stopped, for they were impinging on very delicate ground. Helen knew very well what was
in her own mind,—it would not have found expression from her lip, even if she had not seen
Blanche's agony, lest something would fall from
her not as her idea, but as the popular belief,
which would crush her hopes and sink her soul
in the depths of black despair. Helen understood her cousin and spared her, and Blanche had
a further respite, and laid the ghost of thought .
which was agony to her, that she and Merlin
might be too sib for marriage. The knock at
the door informing them that the carriage was
waiting, and that Mrs. Power was quite ready to
take her drive, caused this earnest conversation
to cease, as the tears rose to the eyes of Blanche,
happy as she was with her visitors, and the prospects for the next few days, for her. Conscious
fears, and a discernment of her cousin's thoughts,
gave poignancy to them, dashed her spirits, and
took away much of her anticipated happiness.
Blanche inherited her father's temperament ;
she had given herself to Merlin, and her determination was now unalterable come weal, come

woe. In this state of mind, she dismissed, as
far as she could, this subject from her thoughts;
and when dressed for outdoor exercise, descended
the noble stairs calm and composed with Helen,
and accompanied Mrs. Power in the carriage for
a beautiful drive through her father's broad domain.

Fred Power had also in the meantime retired
from the breakfast-room, leaving his father and
mother alone to arrange their plans. It was an
idle hour with him, and he walked out alone and
surveyed the broad acres, and meditated on his
prospects. A thought had been instilled in his
mind, which he found it difficult to dismiss,—it
did not make him unhappy, nor did it make him
regret his engagement with Helen Trevernen;
but it made him serious, and cast a cloud athwart
the sunshine of his thoughts, as he walked on
and on, and admired the well-tilled land, acre
after acre receding from his vision as he passed
along by woodland and by stream, by copse
with its gorse cover for foxes and for game, and
common for coursing hares, with open country
for following the exciting sport of fox-hunting;
for the thought still dwelt in his mind and rested
on his soul, that if he were not engaged to the

bright and sparkling Helen Trevernen, it would not be Sir Hugh Laity's fault if he were not engaged to the sedate and amiable Blanche, the heiress of these broad acres. Fred Power was an honourable man—he loved Helen Trevernen, was happy in her society, and admired the qualities of her mind, and, apart from worldly interests, he was satisfied with his choice, and preferred her to Blanche. Fortunately for Helen —quite unknown to her—this reasoning was convincing, and allayed the desire of cupidity, and the very natural feeling of ambition to become powerful and wealthy. Reason now came along the road of thought, and told him that he possessed in Helen Trevernen a treasure of a woman —" and her treasure"—in a word, her love in its very concentrated essence. In Blanche he could not possess this were she by adventitious circumstances compelled, or instigated to betroth herself to him, for she too had a treasure; and that was in keeping by as noble and fine a specimen of manhood as walked the broad earth. Imagination told him, as he continued musing, that fate had not destined him for Blanche, or she for him; for he had been here before, had drunk of the mystic water of St. Ruan's Well, and gave

his heart away to Helen then; and there was
then no Blanche here to interfere with him or
cross his purposes; and so Fred Power became
happy, having ejected unwholesome thoughts,
. and preferred Helen without a dowry to Blanche
the heiress of Tregarthen. If Blanche had not
on his first visit crossed his purpose, certainly a
man very well known, and very much respected
in his sphere of life, now crossed his path; it
was Jenkins, full of bustle and business, who
accosted him with a finger lifted to his hat out
of respect, "and asked how he was, and how
was Miss Helen?" intimating thereby that he
was acquainted with the terms on which he was
visiting here; and, on being answered by the
generous and high-spirited Irishman in a becoming manner, Jenkins told him "he was going
up to stop a badger's hole, that the harriers were
not out to-day, but that he expected the hunts-
man was on the moor, beside Tregarthen Wood,
and that his honour could not do better than
come with him and see the sport, for he
hoped to hunt the badger after he had caught
him, for a grand badger-baiting next week.'
Nothing loth, Fred Power accepted the invitation, and trudged away with Jenkins, forgetting

all his old thoughts, and listening with pleasurable excitement to the boisterous and humorous
descriptions of Jenkins's sporting escapades, in
which he took great delight. They soon fell in
with the hunstsman, and together they went to
the badger's hole. Jenkins was now in his
glory, the hole was stopped, and 'Pincher,' a
celebrated terrier, sent in to face the badger
and drive him out. After an hour's excitement
Power had the satisfaction of seeing the badger
bagged, and poor 'Pincher' doctored for a terrible pinch from the badger. Power gave the
customary tip and retired, leaving the two sporting worthies belonging to Tregarthen to repair
to the 'Rose and Crown' at St. Keverne, and
drink his health, and expatiate on the merits of
dogs in general, and 'Pincher' in particular, and
anticipate the pleasures of the coming badger-
baiting, by discoursing on the qualities of their
favourite dogs and their pluck.

Fred Power's sporting excitement soon disappeared, and he relapsed again into a thinking
mood, and was reflecting on his prospects of
marriage now his father had returned, when
he met Merlin, who was hovering around his
favourite haunts, not knowing what game he

might start, when he, to his surprise, met Fred Power. Hearty was their greeting, and glad were they of this opportunity to cement by intercourse their well-established friendship.

Merlin acknowledged his hopes, almost expectation, of meeting Blanche, as he was rallied by Power, who told him, in a half-serious manner, he must not expect her, as she and Helen were taking a drive with his mother. The conversation now turned on general subjects, and soon Power discoursed freely on his reflections and thoughts when they first met, and imparted to his friend in sincerity his prospects of an early marriage. This led Merlin to reciprocate; and he in return imparted to his friend in sincerity what were his prospects of an early marriage. There was no resemblance between the position of the two men; but it was strange that at the very time Helen and Blanche were in earnest talk on this very subject, in Blanche's boudoir, these two men were confiding in each other, and Fred Power was counselling Merlin to the best of his ability.

Simultaneously with the carriage-drive of the ladies, and the prolonged interview in the woods of these two young men, enjoying each other's society, and rambling over the diversified and extensive Tregarthen estate, Sir Hugh and General Power, arm-in-arm, left the Hall, and were obsequiously bowed out by Bullock. Gently these elderly men walked along the slopes across the park, and along the splendid avenue of trees, where they were sheltered from the noonday sun. Here General Power expressed himself happy, and only here since his return. This implied reference to Lamorna House brought up a sigh from the breast of Sir Hugh, and with it a host of recollections, almost occasioning a remark from him reflecting on Mr. Trevernen, and an inquisitive desire to know the General's opinion of him; but he refrained, and possibly General Power had no particular motive in his observation beyond expressing himself more at home and contented at the Hall than at Mr. Trevernen's, which was very natural.

General Power in his conversation adverted on the distressed and turbulent state of Ireland, and intimated that after his return from London he should, he believed, take up his abode in the neighbourhood.

"And be a neighbour of mine," said Sir Hugh, with gladness; "you are just the man we want here to fill up a vacancy for a rubber at whist."

"But I am thinking what I shall do with Fred," said the General; "and I feel I may confer with you the more freely as we are likely to become members of the same family."

"Good Heavens!" said Sir Hugh; "you don't mean to say that? Well, I like the lad, and did from the first. Modest lad, modest lad. I respect him for it, though he needn't have been so timid, for I have given him every encouragement, and every reason to feel that it would not be disagreeable to me, and I am not the man to make a promise to the ear and break it to the hope. But Blanche; why, she has never hinted anything of the kind to me—and there is every confidence between us—but perhaps a little reserve for the time is but natural, although there was no occasion for it, my Blanche. I will wait your time, my daughter, for your confession, it will not take me now by surprise."

The two men looked in each other's faces with amazement, and there was a pause. Sadness was pictured in each countenance, whilst a guttural utterance came from the General, resembling sounds, to the effect that there must be some mistake. Both men in a moment understood each other, and they knew what each other desired. Immediately the General quickly added,—

"I thought you knew all about it. I knew nothing of it until my arrival, when I was introduced to Helen Trevernen as my future daughter-in-law."

"Helen Trevernen!" exclaimed Sir Hugh; "I never dreamt of it!"

He looked away, and around him in confusion; but quickly his composure was restored by his attention being arrested by a couple of the feathered tribe busy in their world of instinct. He then quietly said, pointing to their loving labour of nidification,—

"Courtship and marriage will go on without my concerning myself about them," and dropped this subject, which had evidently caused him great pain, by stating "that his niece Helen is a good and clever girl, and will make an excellent wife."

General Power, not feeling inclined to extend his walk, and intimating a desire to return to attend to some business connected with his journey to London, returned to the Hall alone.

Sir Hugh was glad to find himself thus situated, so that he might have leisure, in the solitude of his own grounds, to reflect on many subjects which now agitated him. His first thoughts

were concerning his business relations with his
brother-in-law ; these he found on analysis very
unsatisfactory, so the further consideration of
them was put off for a more convenient season.
His next thought was on the discovery he had
now made. He blamed himself for being so
simple and so short-sighted. He blamed Blanche
for not telling him, as she ought to have done,
for he made her his second self, and confided to
her all his mind. "But have I ?" he said, and
the accusing thought of not having done so, out
of consideration to spare her feelings, arose in
his mind when he remembered that he had, if
not entirely, certainly to every useful purpose, abstained from telling her of his disastrous speculations with her uncle, and the inroads he had
made on the old undisturbed family property.
But now the agonizing thought forced itself on
him, " What if Blanche has designedly kept back
the information of her cousin's engagement, fearing it might lead to unhappy disclosures concerning herself ?" And he remembered forcibly, and
with agony, the manner of Blanche when Merlin
jumped into the carriage at the Doctor's, and the
impression it then made on his mind. " What
if," he said aloud, " if she and Merlin have fallen

in love with each other? Nothing more natural, kin with kin." And then he called to mind the meeting at Malta, and the voyage to England on board the 'Hercules.' "My God!" he exclaimed aloud, as his anguish burst forth in great bubbles of sweat upon his brow, "what if I have unconsciously favoured such a catastrophe by my illconcealed partiality for Merlin? Oh, I dread, I fear I have been misunderstood, and my Blanche has misinterpreted my every act towards Merlin. Oh, I had intended my Blanche to marry young Power, with her inheritance, and my Merlin his sparkling and witty cousin Helen, with my personal property at my death, when the grave would have covered my shame, and prevented the blush from rising to my guilty but repentant cheek."

In this frame of mind he hurried, with more than his wonted measured steps, to the cottage, to confer with old Kitty, and deposit there this time, not remorseful and repentant feelings, but his serious misgivings, which had intruded themselves on his mind, and which were not without foundation. Whilst he was hurrying on, in another and more frequented part of his extensive domain, to wit, the carriage-drive, there was a meeting, partly accidental, partly contrived, and partly foreseen. Blanche and Helen certainly had an impression that certain friends of theirs were very likely to be in the wood at this time, and a very clear perception of the paths they would select, in case they by accident met, and this expectation was provocative of an overflow of animal spirits when they entered the carriage, and joined Mrs. Power for a drive. Fred and Merlin also knew that there was a carriage and pair being driven along the carriage-drive, and that if it left the Hall-door, and went eastward, by describing a circle it would necessarily return to the Hall-door from the westward. Taking the hour of noon for starting, and the pace about eight miles an hour, by mathematical calculation to Fred Power, and by nautical observation, navigational conclusion, and seamanship experience to Merlin ; also by earnest deliberation, and a comparison of their respective data of calculation and observation, they both came to the same conclusion, after allowing fractions of time, and inches of space for differences of calculation, that at a certain spot within a furlong either way to the wood on the right, the park on the left, or the road front and back, if they occupied that spot, apart from every other on the round globe at this juncture of time, it was possible, it was probable, nay, it amounted almost to an absolute certainty, that they might fall in with the said carriage, with its fair occupants, on the *ground* from which these curious calculations had been based. They were confirmed in their calculations; they were as true as the needle to the pole, and the planet in her orbit.

"Here they are," said Merlin and Power, as the carriage drove up.

"Here they are," whispered Blanche to Helen.

"Just as I thought," said Helen; "I fain was compelled to believe that a man who could conduct the fast-sailing revenue cutter across St. George's Channel, would not fail to pilot his own love-freighted barque to some such a point as this, and at such a moment."

"Helen, you are incorrigible," said Blanche, with a hearty laugh.

This merriment proceeding from high spirits, would have had on Mrs. Power the effect of dissipating any doubts of this not being an accidental meeting, could they by any possibility have entered her mind, which was not at all likely, as she had been expatiating on the beauties of the park, and the deliciousness of the day,

and her happiness with her two gay and spirited
girls. Mrs. Power had ingratiated herself; she
had been young, and took it upon herself now to
insist that her two girls should get out and walk,
that it would do them more good than riding;
and so, without more ado, Blanche and Helen
tripped down from the carriage, and then tripped
away, leaving Mrs. Power to continue and finish
her drive alone, and to continue expatiating without let or hindrance. She did so, and undoubt-
edly indulged in her complacent reveries until
she arrived at the hall-door entrance from an opposite road to that she left by, as demonstrated
by scientific calculation unknown to her.

Delicious moments now; there was exuberance of joy and happiness, more than compen-
sating for any sadness of the past by separation.
The evening walk along the seashore at the cove
in the moonlight was ecstasy; but now, in the
broad daylight, surrounded with familiar and
enchanting scenery, sequestered from the world,
in the midst of minstrelsy from the wooded song-
sters, life seemed to these happy lovers as if it
were made up of bliss, and they drank deep
draughts of delight afforded by this occasion,
until their very reasons were bewildered, and they

imagined they were in Paradise regained. One
little cloud came sailing along, not bigger than a
man's hand; it was within the limit of their
horizon, and they were therefore affected by it.
It obstructed the sun, and cast its shade along
their thoughts. It was expanding, and darken-
ing by its expanse; and now they knew that this
was not life, and to be happy is to be active;
and that scenes like this must be transient to
be beneficial; few and far between, like angels'
visits, to hallow time, and clothe eternity in rest.
This is a busy working world. Helen knew it,
and they felt it to be so; and they all thought it
wise to make the most of this transient occasion,
before the cloud grew, and on they went lovingly,
as lovers do, until they came, where they had all
often been before under different circumstances,
to old St. Ruan's Well. Here they rested from
their walk, and here they sat down together
under the shadow of a clump of trees, sheltered
from the sun, and listened to the murmuring
music of the overflowing stream from the old
mystic well. Here they chatted over the memories of other days. Blanche remembered it
as a place of awe, and to be shunned in her childhood when she plucked wild flowers, and visited

old Kitty with her father. Merlin remembered
it under similar circumstances, and called to mind
the many times he passed it in going and coming
from school, and pointed out the place in the
adjacent leet where he set his night-lines, baited
with minnows, to catch trout, and expressed his
anxiety and his hope that when he returned to
examine his bait, he might find he had been successful, and pointed his moral that these feelings
gave way to others as boyhood came on, with
his rivalries, and manhood with his feelings at
Aboukir; and then turning to Blanche, he
reminded her of their meeting here and their
betrothal. Power, too, remembered his being
brought here, and the old distich from the
sibyl, as he called her, and inquired if she
were still alive. Blanche and Merlin admo-
nished him, and enjoined silence by placing
their fingers on their lips. More or less super-
stitious by nature, Power felt the loneliness of
the place, and half believed there was a spell
about it, by his compliance with the request, and
his forbearance to either mention old Kitty's
name, or speak disrespectfully of her. Blanche
and Helen sang snatches of duets together; and
such was the loveliness of the well, and the

charm that hung about it, that, not contented
with singing snatches of songs after their duets,
each in turn, as memory served or fancy in-
spired, they culminated this celebration of their
visit by dancing a cotillon to the measure of their
own minstrelsy, accompanied with the music of
the bubbling stream from the mystic well. In
the midst of the dance Blanche uttered a scream ;
in the scream were the words, "My father!"
and immediately she fainted. "What can it
be ?" "What can it mean ?" were sentences
eagerly spoken and unanswered. "I saw no one,"
was said by all, as they laid her down on the
grass under the clump of trees. Power ran from
the well, where the flowing water was easily ac-
cessible, and fetched a little in the palms of his
hands, as well as bringing his pocket-handkerchief dripping wet. The application of the water
revived Blanche, and she became conscious. The
first words she uttered were a repetition of the
scream, "My father, I saw him pass !"

The terrors of her mind were apparent and
uncontrollable, and the cause known to all.
Poor Merlin ! his mind was sadly agitated ; from
a wild excess of almost delirious but thoughtless
delight, it was instantaneously plunged into grief

and hopeless despair, for he saw into the recesses
of his beloved Blanche's soul, and he saw her
fear and dread for the consequences of her engagement with him ; but he rallied her, and gradually
she became more composed, and evidently was
making up her mind to meet her father's dis-
pleasure when he, as she expected, in anger would
upbraid her for permitting Merlin to pay her
attentions and of her becoming engaged to him.
Resting on the green sward, with tears falling
for her relief, and receiving every consolation it
was possible for her friends to bestow, Fred
Power bethought him of going down to the
bottom of the well in the hope that he might find
there some little vessel to bring a little water for
Blanche to drink.  As he approached the curb-
stone and was about to look down from thence,
instead of going round to the opposite side where
the stone winding steps led down to the bottom,
he sprang back in affright, as he heard the sounds
of a human voice ascending from the very bottom.  The sounds were so low and plaintive that,
on his looking at his companions, he noticed that
they had not reached to that distance, as they
remained unconscious of any interruption.  Power
now cautiously stole up to the circular curb-

stones, about three feet high, and looked down the well. At the bottom, very much concealed, he saw a human figure, mantled in a red cloak, apparently with the head almost floating on the surface of the water and drinking the turbid bubbles. Without further motion of the body the well-known voice of old Kitty was heard. Power now sprang over to his companions to prepare them for what was coming, but his intentions were of no avail, although with great dramatic and pantomimic action he caused them to approach him, which they did in terror, not knowing what could be the cause of such agitation. With affrighted countenances all looked down the well, both Merlin and Power being prevented from descending by their required assistance to support the two terrified and half-fainting girls. Hardly had their visions reached the bottom before their ears met old Kitty's voice ascending, plaintive and more musical than ever. She chanted the following rhymes,—evidently improvised :—

"Again at the Well now together ye are,
    Still bidding defiance to kind warning and love ;
The small cloud in the sky, though distant and far,
    Will break in destruction and descend from above.

"Your hour is transient, then make the most of it here,
　All warning you've scouted, now go to your doom;
Still dance your pet dances, and in sweet voices clear
　Sing your glad songs, for to-morrow is gloom!

"The turbulent bubbles will burst on the stream,
　When swollen with water after torrents of rain;
Your phantomized Paradise will fade like a dream,
　And show you your follies in torture and pain!

"For yon girl of quick wit and her gay Irish lover,
　There's blessings in store when these troubles are
　　　past;
But for Blanche and her lover it's my fate to discover,
　That unto life's end their sorrows will last!

"But list to the charm, if you'd be free from your
　　　troubles,
　Ascending in hope from the turbid, burst bubbles:
' Let Blanche and Fred Power inherit the dower,
　And Helen and Merlin inherit the sterling!'"

"Gracious heavens," said Merlin, "I can stand
no more of this;" and releasing his hold of
Blanche and resigning her to Helen, he sprang
down the steps and met his grandmother, who
had arisen from her recumbent position now she
had finished her malediction, and who was quite
prepared for the meeting, as she stood erect and
without heeding Merlin continued ascending to
the surface in calm dignity.

But she was unable to accomplish this, and the

the only words she deigned to utter were, " Not here, my son, not here ;" and such was her commanding mien that she passed Merlin, and passed upwards and away alone.

Merlin quickly followed her, and impatiently demanded knowing why she had been a spy on their walk through the woods, as well as a reason for her outrageous conduct and mysterious manner she had chosen to affect, inspiring awe by singing her doleful and nonsensical rhymes. " I tell you, grandmother," he said, " I'll have no more of it. For myself I do not so much mind, but for Blanche's sake, on whom I know that your mystical demeanour makes a very sad impression, I do resent it. Her peace of mind is very dear to me. You must know that she has engaged to become my wife, and I will not have her peace disturbed or her fears excited by your overbearing manner. Tell me, grandmother, I ask you again,—I implore you to tell us now, all friends, all deeply interested, what is there so mysterious hanging over our heads ? What spell is there that your heated fancy has conjured up against us, and which you seem ill-disposed yourself to break, and would endeavour to prevent our trying to do ? What do you know of me, my birth and

my parentage ? for here is the spell, here is the
demon of wickedness. Is it that I am of so
ignoble a pedigree as to be excluded from an
alliance with the heiress of Tregarthen ?"

"Not too ignoble, my son," was serenely
spoken by old Kitty, "but too "—

"Too what, grandmother ?" rashly spoke
Merlin, giving old Kitty a precious opportunity
for extricating herself from the pressure of his
interrogations, for she would have uttered in her
extremity, "but too near in kindred," and but
for Merlin's passionate impetuosity she would
in her strait have parted with the key to the
mystery of his birth, at the cost of agony and
despair to both Merlin and Blanche.

Old Kitty now resumed her character of sibyl,
and waved her hands in air with a scoffing and
contemptuous expression, repeated her last words,
and changed their sentiment into " too hasty and
too violent."

Merlin now discovered his mistake, and regretted his impulsive precipitancy, believing he
had thereby lost an opportunity of finding the
thread which would unravel the mystery of his
life. He knew his grandmother's temperament,
and was silent. She gradually receded from

view, expressing a command that, as in the cotillon just danced they changed partners, so they
should change partners for life, and then curses
should be turned into blessings, and old St. Keverne should ring a merrier peal than had been
rung for many a day. This request fell like a
clap of thunder on the astonished listeners, who
were now within hearing. Helen now fairly gave
way, and wept with Blanche, who was speechless
with dismay. Homewards they went; a little
cloud had sprung up, and it was expanding.
Blanche now could not scare away her sorrow and
her fear, and Merlin trembled as he never had
before,—no, not in battle, not in storm! It was,
however, arranged between this peace-disturbed
party as they walked towards the Hall that it
would be wise to be as equable in their temperament as usual, and not to invite the expected
storm from Sir Hugh. Possibly it might not
break, and possibly it might pass away.

Sir Hugh was sitting in the porch on his accustomed seat, waiting for old Kitty, when she
returned flurried from her visit to the well, in
sight of which he passed on his way, and but for
his being absorbed in thought must have been
attracted to it by the familiar forms and voices

he might have seen and heard. It was likely therefore that Blanche saw her father pass when she screamed, but he heeded not, for he, like the old well, was full to overflowing after rain in torrents. Little Beda was unceremoniously sent away, when immediately Sir Hugh began to recount his troubles and his fears, and demanded what old Kitty knew, very peevishly and very authoritatively.

She now frankly told him of his daughter's engagement with Merlin and the course she had pursued, repeating the last rhymes she had so lately uttered, and describing the scene at the well she had but now left. Sir Hugh's feelings were very acute, his grief was very poignant, his reproaches on himself heart-rending. Old Kitty silenced his objurgations, and bade him not to be so cast down; more, she consoled him with all her inventive persuasion, and told him that yet there was a chance of defeating the dreaded catastrophe of a union with Blanche and Merlin. She repeated to him her warning at the well, and said she had so discomposed them with her malediction and astonished them with her commands to exchange partners for life that they were struck dumb with amazement. "I have thrown in the apple of discord. I shall set on the young wasp, Evered, and you let my charm work, Sir Hugh."

"It is vile,—it must never be," he despairingly said.

"It is the only hope, Sir Hugh. When this charm is worked out, I have done; and for me, they may then rush on to their doom. But oh, my dear master, let old Kitty yet plead with you; let her have one more chance, and then, if she fail, let the storm burst. But, in the meantime, be calm, serene,—be yourself,—take no notice,— play the host, and don't cease loving my dear Blanche, and don't blame Merlin! But get him to sea again, and I'll use the self-willed Evered by flattering him, and will set him on to poison Power's mind against Helen, and persuade him that Merlin has been affected towards her ever since their voyage from Ireland, for I have heard of her admiration of his command, and her being with him in the dead of night on the deck in the storm. What more natural?"

"And what then?" said Sir Hugh, with intense agitation, as he perceived the unscrupulous scheme of his old and faithful dependant had been driven to adopt in her extremity.

"What then?" repeated old Kitty. "Why then, having used my young traitorous schemer for my own purposes, I will set Power on to Blanche, and persuade her to forget Merlin. Oh, it goes against me, but if this will not save them, nothing will; and if my charm should work, why their destiny is averted and their happiness secured. This end, Sir Hugh, must justify the means." And old Kitty had finished.

Sir Hugh believed on old Kitty, and hoped her desperate cause would be successful; he determined to be very circumspect, and as soon as Merlin was away again at sea, to hasten General Power's departure and accompany him to London, leaving destiny to shape her ends, rough hewn by one who had dropped unwittingly into this strange situation stage by stage.

Dr. Fergus had called at the Hall; finding all out, he left his regards and apologized for not stopping, as he and 'Scrubby' were very busy and were like the muleteer, "they had many a mile to go."

# CHAPTER VIII.

"IAGO.  That Cassio loves her, I do well believe it,
That she loves him 'tis apt, and of great credit."
' *Othello.*'

GREAT preparations were now making for the
wrestling-match to take place on Goonhilly
Downs.   It was not a county match exactly, but
confined to the western division of the county;
and although eastern men were not expected to
compete for the prizes, which were the results of
local subscription, yet they were not ineligible,
and one or two would be welcomed and possibly
invited, so as to give zest and variety to the
contest.   The two divisions in these matches
were distinct; it was only in the great county
matches where and when the distinction did not
appear, and all men who chose competed, and
young men tried their skill and courage, and

tested their powers publicly in earning their half-crowns, in becoming standards or eligible to wrestle for the prizes.

Just at this time, to Jenkins' disgust, his mother-in-law intimated a desire to her daughter Jenny that she wanted to go into Pendeen, and that Jenkins must drive her in one of the farm carts; and not contented with this direction, so fully was she acquainted with the resources of the farm that she desired a very favourite mare called 'Charlotte,' should be used for the purpose. This also put Jenkins out of temper when he was told of it by his faithful partner, Jenny, because it so happened the mare was at this time nursing mother of a very fine colt, which Jenkins was taking especial care of for the next agricultural show, and to allow the colt to run by the side of its mother to and from Pendeen, or leave it at home unnursed, was in his eyes a serious matter, and could he have expressed himself, would have been as gross a piece of vandalism as ever was perpetrated, but not knowing anything about the history of the Vandals, and not being accustomed to ride the high horse, he simply grumbled and growled, and very properly so. As Jenny told him " it was abominable," but nevertheless

Charlotte must go, so Jenny like a wise woman
gave her Samson his supper, hot, strong, and
warm, and very soon the grumble declined to a
mumble, and at the appointed time Jenkins with
the mare Charlotte in the cart, were beside the
cottage ready to take Old Kitty into Pendeen.
What her object was, never occurred to Jenkins.
Charlotte the mare was his object of thought, and
whether or not Bob the ploughboy would mind
the colt and give it the milk warm and in sufficient quantity. Old Kitty was pleased at her .
wishes or request having been respected, for she
knew Charlotte's condition and her son-in-law's
feelings, and because of this she was very gracious
to Jenkins, and complimented him on Charlotte,
and talked about the colt at home, and hoped
Bob would mind it; if he didn't she would see
that he should not be spared the next time he was
absent from the Sunday school and went bird-
nesting instead, or made a noise in church; she
would see that the rod should not be spared; all
of which talk was very annoying to Jenkins.
He wanted to forget the colt now, and did not in
the least understand his mother-in-law, or what
she was about, which was in truth exercising a
little authority of mind or intellect over inert

matter and body.   Old Kitty was kind-hearted,
and respected Jenkins ;  he was a good husband
in his way, and had a talent she appreciated ;  he
was slow to speak, and was as well trained as
any of his dogs, and never gave tongue except
when Jenny abused her privileges, and provoked
his wrath by keeping him waiting for his meals.

Old Kitty changed the conversation to a theme
not only congenial, but within the horizon of her
son's bounded intellect, and talked of the wrestling, inquired if he had been in practice and in
training, and then again " touched him on the
raw," as he gave a least touch of his whip to
Charlotte, when she supposed he did not now
drink anything, but strictly dieted himself.

Now Jenkins' idea of training was not to cut off
his beer, he had an idea that it was the right
thing.   Old Kitty always made her plaister
broader than the sore, physically so, for she was
almost Dr, Fergus's rival, but figuratively, as she
approved of her son's system of diet and preparation, and testified her sincerity by giving him her
steel-ringed purse, for they were approaching
Pendeen, and requesting him to use as much as
he required for refreshment, she was too proud
to allowance him, remarking that there was

enough there and perhaps a shilling or two over, which, if not used, he could return with the purse at 5 o'clock when she would be ready to go home, and waiting for him at the bottom of the street leading out of the town. This was all quite clear and perfectly within the bounds of Jenkins' comprehension. The purse was heavy; in fact, it was a handsome tip of the old lady, and kindly done, as Jenkins admitted, so Charlotte was whipped up with a will, and Jenkins showed his pleasure like a child with a toy. This again tickled the old woman and fed her vanity, and was a provocative to chide him as she would a child, which she did, and which he did not discover, for he had got the money, and smiled on his mother-in-law such a smile of satisfaction and honest-hearted submission to her will, that the tear came into her eye, and she could hardly suppress it when she said, " If you beat Charlotte so, I must take away the purse."

"No, no, granny," he said, "it is in my grip now;" and his handsome but tanned, whiskered face uncouthly bent itself downwards and kissed the now wrinkled but once handsomest face in the county.

This act put the old lady in her gayest mood,

and she descended from her conveyance at the entrance of the town, and clad in her own peculiar costume passed through it in dignity, where in years now gone by, when a girl, she had flirted her gay and winsome hours away, and danced her measure on the green with the best of them.

Old Kitty had a day's work before her, and one end in view in coming; she paid many visits to old cronies, and some visits to old tradespeople who had done business at the Hall time out of mind. Gradually she wound her way towards Mr. Trevernen's office, passing the Institution and making a call there, for she was known there, but not finding the object of her search, after inviting the housekeeper and her children to come out and junket with her, saying, "that little Beda would be glad to see the children," she left, and proceeded further, until at last she arrived at the office and saw the names, "Trevernen and Son" on the brass plate at the door.

"By my sooth," she thought, "this is a fine office. I hope they haven't got too much of my dear master's money, but I fear too much of it is here about; and, my stars! what is that below? 'Great Pendeen Consols Mining Company's

Office.' Here are great pretensions and I fear
bad results. Shall I stay here or go in? but I
have no errand."

Fortunately whilst thus meditating, Evered
stepped out; he caught her eye in a moment,
paused, and then, like a bird careering in mid air
fascinated with the call bird, stooped and flew,
irresistibly attracted, into the net prepared to
receive him. Possibly business thoughts at the
moment of his leaving the office occupied his
mind, but in another there was a complete change
by the law of association, and his soul became
flooded with feelings of unrequited love, hate, revenge, and curiosity to know what brought old
Kitty here : and with an instantaneously formed
resolution to enlist her sympathies and employ
her in some scheme, which at that moment was
only conceived, so quick was the intellect of
Evered Trevernen, and so ripe for mischief.

He accosted her. After the usual greeting of
its kind, Evered was allowed to discover that
there was motive and design in old Kitty's being
in Pendeen, concealed as it might be,—he pierced
through that veil and immediately assumed he
was the cause, and like a woodcock to a spring,
so went Evered to it, and old Kitty had only to

let him alone, and she did. There were a few
moments of earnest conversation; suddenly it
ceased, and he parted from her with loud accents.
" Well, I am glad to see you, Kitty, who would
have thought of seeing you here, but you must
not go back without paying us a visit at Lamorna
House; mamma would indeed be disappointed if
you did not;" and having graciously dismissed
her he went to soliloquize, and crack a nut old
Kitty had put into his mouth.

Old Kitty's object had been attained; there
was now no need of her going up to the house;
however she went, and was warmly received by
Mrs. Trevernen, and duly honoured. She was a
true Laity, and in old Kitty's eyes had demeaned
herself by marriage to a merchant. The man
with the land and a coat-of-arms on his carriage,
was a man after old Kitty's own heart to honour;
she could do obeisance to him, though he were a
fool and a slave to every habit. It was her weak-
ness.

The visit between Mrs. Trevernen and old
Kitty was an agreeable one, and they talked a
great deal. Wine and cake were brought up by
Sally, the parlour maid, who told cook in the
kitchen, with whom she was on very confidential

terms at this time, that "for her part she did not know what there could be in that old fortune-teller upstairs, to engage her mistress so much that she didn't even know when she came in with the tray, but the artful, cunning, old impostor did. She had her weather eye open, and ears too, for the matter of that, for I couldn't catch a word they were talking about, for she muddled her mistress's talk so when she entered, that I am sure the old gipsy must have been telling her fortune; and if she hadn't have looked so grandiferous and proud, I would have waited outside until she went, and have asked her down, and we would club round and have our fortunes told too, for I'm sure she can do it. Oh, Barbara, I'm sure she can do it, for she looked like the witch in the fender when the king was showed his murdered wife's face in the fire."

" Sally," said Barbara, the cook, " it is not so. It is the witch of Hender with Samuel and Saul fighting in a glass, it's in the Bible."

"Well, I only say what I always heard, Barbara, and I don't believe you have no more a' read it than me, now, that I don't; pretending to know what's in your Bible. I never see you a-reading it, nor nobody else for that, they've all got one I know, upstairs and downstairs, but I never see any one read out of it. I only hear it read at church every Sunday, and I expect I'm just like the rest. But oh, Barbara, I should like to have my fortune told. I'm sure I shall have a sailor, for I always crawl to the basin of water every Christmas Eve when we try our fortune, and I always dream when it's stormy weather of that handsome Mr. Hay Bee what came up here with Mr. Merlin when Miss Helen came home from Ireland. I'm sure he's called Mr. Hay Bee, Barbara, so don't conterdict me. I heard Mr. Merlin say when they was a-talking about his crew, and Miss Helen asked him about this very one; because he asked her to drink in the storm, and said she ought to be a sailor's bride; and he said, 'Yes, yes, I know the man, he's a Hay Bee.' I'm sure he called him so; don't be so stupid, Barbara, he did say so, and that's his name, for what else could he mean. And just fancy," she said running off to answer the bell, " being asked in church (sailors are always called Jack, so he must be called Jack), Jack Hay Bee, bachelor, to Sally Lovewell, spinster; this is for the first time of asking; I'm sure I should faint."

Barbara laughed at her fellow-servant's conceit

and went about her work, Sally to answer the
bell and show old Kitty out,—for she had by this
time paid her visit, talked with Mrs. Trevernen
about old times and about present times, and
now was prepared to take her leave.

Sally, it may be remarked, was not accustomed to pay particular attention to her pronun-
ciation; had she been a little more familiar with
her mother-tongue, possibly she would have
avoided the confusion her mind fell into when she
heard Merlin reply to Helen Trevernen's question
about this sailor who had struck her fancy so,
that he was neither captain nor coxswain, but
simply an A. B., meaning thereby an able-bodied
seaman. Sally, however, not hearing the whole
of the conversation heard only A. B., and concluded that articulation had reference to the
sailor's name, which finally fixed itself in her
mind, her dreams, hopes, fears, and fortune-
telling, as Mr. Hay Bee.

Sally was strongly tempted to make an overture to old Kitty, but her courage failed her, and
perhaps it was best that it did, for it saved her a
rebuke and old Kitty from vexation.

The hour for her departure had now arrived,
she had accomplished her mission, and punctual

to time she found Jenkins at the appointed place
and was driven home in good humour by Charlotte,
the milky mother of as fine a colt as the county
could produce, or at least, Jenkins told his mother-
in-law so, going home; but then the purse had
been returned, and old Kitty noticed without remark, that it was now as light as it well could be,
and Jenkins as foggy as he ought to be to drive
his favourite Charlotte. However, they all got
home in good time, and Jenkins took his supper,
after he was satisfied that Bob had taken care of
the colt, and Charlotte was restored to her
maternal obligations; an old and certain proof to
Jenny, by this inverted arrangement on the part
of her husband, that he was not very hungry, but
very possibly "three sheets in the wind," a very
equivocal but well-understood proverbial expression in the district.

The following morning St. Keverne church town
was alive with bustle and excitement; the wrest-
ling-day was approaching, and the 'Rose and
Crown' was filled and emptied again and again
throughout the day by earnest inquirers after information. Jenkins, the representative man of St.
Keverne, with others—chiefly young fishermen
from the coves adjacent—were there in earnest

conversation, surrounded with old and retired wrestlers, receiving from them hints and instructions. The chief cause for excitement in the conversation arose from the announcement that Gundry, a young man of middling stature but of immense endurance, and rising into notoriety, belonging to Redruth, was to compete. Some thought that he ought to be excluded, as being out of the district; others believed that he would carry off the prize, and therefore they were loud in disclaiming his pretensions to wrestle.

Merlin and Power strolled down to the village, having met by appointment, and whilst there to their surprise fell in with Evered Trevernen. He was in full chat with the wrestlers, freely giving his opinion as to the issues of the coming match. After the usual courtesies and inquiries, Evered asked if they intended witnessing the wrestling, and being answered in the affirmative, he accepted an invitation to join them, and make one of a party. Merlin also told him that he had granted permission to his men to wrestle, and he supposed some of them would indulge in their fancy, and therefore he felt it his duty to be present. Having drunk a glass of mine host's home-brewed and best sparkling ale, with a mouthful of bread and cheese, and thereby giving *éclat* to the coming contest by coming in contact with the villagers and fishermen, they parted,—Merlin to superintend his duties on board his cutter, accompanied by Power, and Evered to walk on to the cottage of old Kitty Keskeys, in consequence of the few earnest words that evidently passed between them yesterday when they met at Pendeen.

What were the thoughts of Evered as he walked from St. Keverne to the cottage, and what were his feelings as he passed the cross roads which led to the Hall, and where he was interrupted by Jenkins' sudden appearance from pressing further his suit to the unwelcome ear of his cousin Blanche ?—who can tell ? But doubt-less his mind was full of thought and feeling, and very suspicious of old Kitty's sincerity and good intentions towards him. But if he discovered treachery, he would—well, by this time he arrived, and he had no immediate occasion to resolve what he would do if he really found that she was only making use of him to serve other ends. This state of mind, occasioned by brooding over his position and plans, made Evered meet old Kitty with a serious and severe expression of countenance, which had the effect of preventing any cant or hypocrisy. He entered the cottage and took his seat, and at once began the conversation, taking the lead and assuming a manner hostile and offensive. He said—

"Kitty, I believe you hate me, and that it is not for love you have enticed me here; but you must have your plans, and if they suit with mine, why we may like dogs hunt in couples, each to our end. I do not know for certainty who Merlin is, but I tell you I hate him and always did,—he has always crossed my path. I tell you, also, that I love my cousin Blanche, and I will compass heaven, earth, and hell, but what I'll have her, or be her ruin! I tell you I believe Merlin loves her, and here he crosses my path in the most fearful way one man can another. So, Kitty, let's have none of your fortune-telling,— you may spae a fortune for aught I know, and you may bamboozle silly women for aught I care, but that nonsense won't do with me, I can tell you. I have told you my feelings,—now tell me your secret plans. You came to entice me here, and here I am, old beldame!"

"Have you done?" coolly said old Kitty. "Very well, now don't interrupt me, you villainous young wasp, but let me endeavour to make an honest man of you. Merlin must not marry Blanche—there are reasons; the time has come when steps must be taken to prevent it, and it depends on yourself whether I—yes, Kitty Keskeys—will aid you or another. Merlin must be provided for, but not after your fashion, and there is only one way,—by leading him off the road which leads to Blanche, and directing him on the road to Helen."

"Helen!" exclaimed the exasperated Evered, " my sister?—never!"

"Stay, infuriated fool, or I'll blast your hopes for ever! I say Helen,—Helen Trevernen, your sister, her equal and her appropriate husband; and by your behaviour will be determined the interest I take in you, to help you to be preferred before Power, whose attentions will very soon be transferred to Blanche, as the Irish voyage has disturbed old engagements, for Helen now is smitten with Merlin through that eventful voyage, and Power sees it, and intends to change partners, as he has seen the heiress and admires her barony. Merlin, I can assure you, Sir, is strangely affected towards Helen; he is dazzled by her winning ways, and is like a moth hovering around a flame, ready to be consumed by her fascination, and is more in love with her than Blanche, although he doesn't know it."

" Ho, that's it !" sarcastically said Evered, for the moment charmed and tamed.

" Well, never mind him," said Kitty, " but strive like a man to win your cousin. You are a Laity by your mother's side, and ought to have a better chance than Power, and will have, if it is not ruthlessly destroyed by your jealous and envious conduct towards Merlin. Ah, I see you apprehend me."

" What will you have me to do ?" said Evered.

" Do ?" said Kitty, " do nothing until Power has quarrelled with Helen."

" And then he flies to Blanche !" said Evered with scorn and fury on his lips.

" True," said old Kitty, " but will the proud Blanche condescend to accept Helen's transferred lover, who is not comparable to Merlin ? Certainly not !—it is impossible ; and then the out-raged Blanche will resent the Irishman's advances, and in a pet he will fly off to Ireland with his blood in a boil at his stupidity, and then your opportunity may come, and you may make an impression on your cousin and win her whilst the tear is in her eye."

Old Kitty knew she had gone as far as she could with approval to her conscience,—perhaps further. She knew but despised the Jesuitical doctrine of doing evil that good may come,—there was no Christianity in it, and she despised herself, but she had now wound up her charm and set it a-going, however much her tool affected to despise her fortune-telling; having done so, she was mute and so was Evered, and there was a moment's silence. Evered rose to go, and pierced her through with his eyes. He paused before her with his hat on his head, his countenance quivering with agitation. At last he was able to speak—

"I understand you," he said, "but if you forsake me, and help Power to Blanche's affections, I'll tear you limb from limb, and will shoot Merlin, though I hang for it before the county jail!" With this expressed determination he left abruptly.

Grave reflections came over old Kitty. That Evered was a villain she knew, and she only used a villain, but that he despairingly loved his cousin she was now convinced of, and pity and compassion were mingled with her thoughts, and she reasoned thus :—" If Merlin and Helen are

united, Evered will have an equal chance with
Power to solace Blanche, and according to his
discretion so should be her advice to Blanche,
which she believed she would have sooner or
later to tender to a broken-hearted girl, and
which in anticipation already distressed her
sorely, for she feared Evered would very soon
discover an opportunity to display his wondrous
mischief-making powers, and not be content to
wait patiently the course of events which she
was endeavouring to bring about.

# CHAPTER IX.

" To-morrow, Sir, I wrestle for my credit."

'*As you Like it.*'

THE morning for the wrestling-match had at last arrived, and the preparations from far and near were ready. At early morn were to be seen pedestrians, carts and horses, waggons and wains conveying people and refreshment. It was a people's gathering, and a day of great expectation,—perhaps of greater excitement than a county wrestling-match. The subscriptions had been liberal, consequently the prizes were worth contending for. Moreover, the morning was beautiful, and there were no doubts or fears regarding the weather which might mar the pleasure and the junketing of the people. The boats were all ashore,—fishes, crabs, and lobsters had a rest as far as Cadgwith, Lamorna, Kynance

Coves with their fishermen were concerned, and all was bustle at early morning with this early-rising population. From all parts were processions of merrymakers hurrying towards the breezy locality of Goonhilly Downs, an old contest field, endeared to the aged, now making their pilgrimages with their descendants now about to contest their powers as they did in the preceding age. Here was the same place unaltered, presenting the same picturesque view of sea and land, varied by hill and dale, stream and river ever flowing, whilst the ages had come and gone, and the populations were following in their wonted course, still evenly flowing on, and will if left alone for ever. Here, on these breezy downs, on the old, old spots, were tents re-erected the same as time out of mind, containing cold provisions for the excited throng, each tent being according to custom fixed in the position nearest to the parish or locality on the Downs to which its owners belonged, and where the athletes of that immediate district made their changes of costume for wrestling, and where they received the attentions requisite after the struggle. They were characterized by flags and by mottoes rudely painted on canvas. For instance, one tent was fitted with deal tables, the forms and chairs possibly borrowed from the accompt houses of adjacent mines, and stocked with barrels of beer, and 'moonshine' in its proper place, to shine at its proper time, and solid victuals. Over its entrance were these uncouth rhymes :—

"'Killigrews' and 'Carnsews,' great wrestlers in their
    day,—
Many a 'fall' they gave, but are fallen to decay;
Men of Rosemullion, who challenge the county over,
Will this day be thrown by the Men of Penolver."

Over the entrance of another booth were these rhymes :—

"Lads of Ruan Minor Poltesco, renowned for their
    strength,
To-day on the downs will measure their length;
For the lads of St. Keverne, with their champion Jenkin,
By the 'crook and foreheap' will throw 'em in a twinkling."

And over the entrance of another, there were the following rhymes :—

"Men of Lelant and St. Ive's, with Kneebone the smelter
    of tin,
Will throw Tom Gundry, and then beg the great ring,
And win the first prize—twenty pounds, so they say—
Then hurra, Cornish boy's, for the wrestlers to-day !"

About the tents and within them partisans of the different sections loitered, but not exclusively

so, for there was great good temper, and many
visits were paid and returned by the curious,—
partly to see the men engaged to wrestle and
form their opinion on their condition and chances
of winning, and partly out of that extraordinary
desire on occasions like this to know and let it
be known that they were on intimate terms with
those concerned.

The morning was now advancing. Many little
circles were constantly forming and breaking up
on the Downs in immediate vicinity to the booths,
created by boys wrestling. Gradually an immense
circle or ring was formed, with children in the
front, sitting or lounging on the heathery fern,
gorse, and white heath which formed the flooring;
also there were baskets of provisions, and every
arrangement that could be improvised to spend
a delightful and exciting day. Gradually, as the
interest deepened and the day crept on, and the
populations all trending from the Land's End
on the west and very considerable distances from
the east, arrived, the ring became composed of a
multitude of many thousands, three or four deep.
There was a pavilion or grand stand for the
committee and quality. Ladies did not attend or
support this county game, but many titled men

from afar came in their carriages, and as
anuounced in a kind of Memoriam over one of
the booths, they once contested for the prizes,—
in a word, they wrestled in the ring with their
dependants; but that day had gone by, and now
the quality only supported wrestling by their
subscriptions and patronized it by their presence.
The old custom was followed in making what
was termed a certain number of "standards,"
that is, fresh men were invited to wrestle, and
every man who could throw two men—of course
one after another—flat on their backs was
dubbed "a standard," and entitled to receive
half-a-crown for such distinction and entitled to
wrestle in the next round, and so on, if not
thrown, in an ever-contracting circle, until there
were but as many left as represented the number
of prizes to be contended for, when the maddening excitement commenced for the contest of the
prizes, as it would now become known who must
have them, but not the first, second, and third
prizes, or as many as might be. The earlier part
of the day was occupied with indifferent wrestlers,
and consequently there was much chaff, coaxing,
and wheedling to get young men to try their
prowess in a public ring. After a while it was

announced a sufficient number of "standards" had been made, which included the men of renown, who had gone through in the course of the day the same ordeal as the new and untried men, and who had thrown small or weakly ones in order to attain to the necessary position, but amidst laughter, as some untried men had knowledge and pluck, and gave trouble to the more professional combatants, to their annoyance but to their popularity, by giving them a kind of standing for the future. A sumptuous lunch having been partaken of by the quality, they arranged themselves in convenient positions, and the real wrestling now began. Hours flew away like moments, and ten thousand heads were strained to one point to see the varying results of two celebrated players who were equally matched.

Dr. Fergus always made it a matter of consequence to attend these matches, but from causes only of importance to himself. His imagination allowed him to see Olympian games, the Roman Amphitheatre, and the gladiators; also, these contests presented to him the splendid anatomy of the human body when in its grandest form, quivering with the intensified soul within it, and every muscle and nerve strained to its utmost, until at last, when overpowered and mastered, it gradually yields its tension, and, quivering for a second, loses its balance, and falls, or rather is thrown, flat on its back. This, to Dr. Fergus, was a sight worth seeing, and always commanded his subscription. More than ordinary excitement was manifested on this occasion, for a new man from Redruth, named Gundry, made his appearance, and from what was known of him it was thought he would prove to be an "ugly customer." Kneebone, a man of immense strength, who could lift two large blocks of tin, but of no brains or science, was present; he had one chance of success, if he could once enfold his man his immense strength was fatal to his rival, generally, however, this was avoided by small men, who, seeing what he was about, caught him by the toe and tripped him up or down, to his amazement, and then crestfallen he had to retire; strength without science was of no avail. The 'Sylvia's' men were here wrestling, and Mr. A.B. was their exponent; he was light, agile, and a very pretty wrestler, his skill was exhibited not in kicking, but in lively action, catching his rival with his toe just at the moment of oscillation, when the weight of the body was being transferred from one leg to the other. Jenkins, of course, was here, the hope of St. Keverne, and the expected winner of the first prize. Unfortunately, in the lots drawn, Jenkins was pitted against A.B., the 'Sylvia's' best man; they were friendly, linked by Merlin to the same section, but so it was, and they were told although it was unfortunate, nevertheless it was expected that each man would do his duty, for it was, after all, but a game of sport. The two poor fellows went in against each other with doleful looks, A.B. saying, " I'm sorry, Jenkins, but I must do my best; there's Nancy at the Hall, she's down at the cove, and will hear all about it."

" Go on," said Jenkins, "do your best, lad, but, mind, whoever is thrown is to give his hand," that is, to be shaken in good will.

With this arrangement they wrestled together and displayed great skill, but it was apparent from the first who would have to give his hand, although Nancy would hear of it, for Jenkins had his eye, not on A.B., he knew his play, and all about him, but on the twenty pounds and that terrible Gundry. Soon Jenkins got warm, forgot all feelings of delicacy, put forth his skill and his

strength at a favourable moment and decked the
sailor, a fair fall was proclaimed by the umpire.
Many friends, and amongst them the sailor's
beloved Merlin, poured in the oil and bound up
the wound of his broken spirit, "Never mind,
Frank," he said, "it is no disgrace for any man
to be thrown by Jenkins, it is an honour to
wrestle with him;" and the simple-hearted sailor
wept, but was out of sorts nevertheless, and re-
fused to be comforted by Jenkins, by his messmates, and by Jenny herself, until he had seen
his Nancy! She did the work; she told him he
wrestled well, all said so, and would have stood
a good chance for the second prize but for the ill-
luck of having to wrestle with Jenkins, who was
the best wrestler in the county. The simple-
hearted Frank, having found he had not fallen by
his fall in his Nancy's estimation, immediately on
parting with her got drunk with a few choice
spirits. Such is life! Jenkins now learnt that
he and Gundry were pitted against each other for
the first and second prizes, and he now knew that
his hour was come. He knew his man, and
knew him to be very wary, and never to give a
chance by a mistake from hastiness or from error,
he knew also he had imperturbable courage and

patience, and felt the assurances of his friends for his success were without foundation, and the directions from Evered Trevernen to go in and win ridiculous. He sent for Merlin, or rather intimated that he would like to see him, and to him in his St. Keverne booth Merlin went. He mentioned to Sir Hugh what had passed between them; it was short, but to this effect, that Jenkins would do his best, but they must not be angry if he were thrown, for the man he was now going to wrestle with was unlike every one else, and would be the champion of the county. Merlin further said, "I have encouraged him, but without avail, for he said, 'it was not fear, nor shame, but a conviction that he had more than his match,' and he told him so as to prevent disappointment."

The excitement when these two athletes entered the arena was unparalleled, the immense crowd was hushed into silence; they were afraid to breathe, so intense were their sympathies. The usual ceremonies were gone through, a little pantomime, a little coquetting, just to know each other's style, was performed, as they had never, until now, wrestled together, and Jenkins was well known throughout the county. Minutes passed away; several bouts to the advantage of neither were skilfully waged, at last, in the twinkling of an eye Gundry seized a chance and closed with his man, equally quick Jenkins counterfoiled it by locking his rival's legs, and thus prevented Gundry turning him over, and if either gave way under these circumstances Jenkins would have been the victor. The wrestling was now maddening excitement to the spectators: for a moment it was all strength, Gundry had found his equal, and tried his utmost to overpower him, but in vain, together they contended in this position, with every nerve and muscle strained to its utmost, to the intense delight of Dr. Fergus; at last the bout ended in a draw, and neither man came off victorious. Jenkins now felt convinced that he would never throw Gundry, and that it was merely a work of time for Gundry to throw him; he was right, for after a protracted struggle it became evident to all that Jenkins would be vanquished, and so the contest ended by a desperate effort made by Jenkins to catch his antagonist in his favourite hold; he was not quick enough, and the wily Gundry caught him instead, and prevented his counterfoiling him a second time. In this supreme and final effort, to

the spectators, time was chained, and the globe's
history in suspense, there was to them the silence
of a depopulated world as they beheld the wonderful machine tented to its utmost, with every
nerve and muscle quivering in the agony of conflict. Existence under this condition must be
with seconds, and endurance with minutes. It
was so. Gradually the muscles of Jenkins re-
laxed, and then he was thrown! The interest
was now over; Gundry won the first prize and
Jenkins the second, and after the concluding
bouts were contested with diminished interest
the prizes were awarded, the speeches of con-
gratulation and condolence made, and the quality
retired, leaving this great assemblage to drink,
quarrel, wrestle little matches, and get home as
well as they could, which they did over many
weary miles late at night or in early morning,
delighted with their day's pleasure, and furnished
with pabulum for conversation and argument for
months and months.

# CHAPTER X.

" IAGO.  But I will wear my heart upon my sleeve
For daws to peck at.   I am not what I am."
*' Othello.'*

MIXED up with the dispersing crowds retiring
from the field of contest were three gentlemen on
horseback, riding rapidly towards Kynance Cove,
they were Merlin, Power, and Evered.    The
' Sylvia' being ready for sea again was lying off
the cove, the nearest point of embarkation, waiting to receive her Commander and the portion of
her crew who had been on shore on leave of
absence, to witness as well as take part in the
great wrestling contest.    In the course of the
day there had been much eager argument between Merlin and Evered, the latter more than
once having assumed a provocative manner,
which was noticed by Merlin, and aroused his

anger, but he restrained it, and thereby avoided any unpleasantness. It was the original intention of Merlin to accompany Sir Hugh back to the Hall, spend a long evening, that is, remain there to the last moment consistent with prudence, and then indulge in a midnight walk and ruminate to his heart's content until he reached his grandmother's cottage, and then leave early in the morning and resume his command, but he altered his mind in the course of the day and resolved to go on board with his crew immediately after the wrestling. Having made this arrangement he dispatched, by a sure hand, a letter to his dear Blanche, informing her of the necessity of his making this alteration in his plans, and also a few lines to the Cottage, informing his grandmother that he should not return, but go direct on board. Having dispatched his letters, he invited his two friends to dine with him on board his cutter, and promised to land them on the following morning at Sennen Cove, some few miles to the westward of Pendeen, where, by directions, a conveyance could be in waiting to take them home. Power and Evered accepted the invitation, and instead of going to the Hall to dine with Sir Hugh, Mr. Trevernen, and General

Power, they accompanied Merlin to Kynance Cove to embark on board the Commander's gig, which would be in waiting there to row them off, accompanied by the large boat used in boarding smugglers to take off the crew. On their road they passed group after group retiring weary, loud in their expression of opinion concerning the match, but of a very incomprehensive manner on account of the drink and the excitement. The sailors were overtaken and passed on the way loudly talking with the stragglers, all of whom were much the worse for drink, and very noisy. Frank, the fancy "Haybee," was not amongst them, some neighbourly Samaritan having taken him into his waggon, where he was lying oblivious to everything and everybody. On their arrival at the cove Merlin intended to wait for his sailors, and then convey his visitors in his gig, but he was overruled, and the care of the large boarding boat was entrusted to the skilful urchin, Master Tommy Dart, who had just before opportunely arrived from the scenes of the wrestling before his Commander, he having heard by accident that he was going off to-night to his dismay and disappointment, for he was supposed to have been at the cove on duty, but instead, he had been in the throng, and dodging his Commander all day ; he was now very cross, and so were the sailors, for this sudden movement had disconcerted their plans, and prevented their making a night of it with Jenkins and his party at the ' Rose and Crown.'   It so happened that there was a ground swell on, and steadiness was essential on the part of the crew.   Merlin now determined to wait until his men assembled, as he saw how matters were tending, although the importunity and almost insulting opinion of its being unnecessary to wait was so persisted in by Evered, accompanied with the information that he was hungry and wanted his dinner, this appeal almost persuaded him to yield to the imperious disposition of Evered, it was, however, well that he did not.   The sailors, through the kindness of the farmers with their traps, were picked up and brought to the cove in much less time than they would have otherwise occupied. Sailors, it may be remarked, are not proverbial for being good walkers, and especially so now as their steps were anything but uniform, and their proceedings anything but under control.   However, sooner than Merlin expected, down they came rollicking and roaring like bulls, and

swearing they would not go on board, but go up
to the 'Rose and Crown.' Merlin, however, was
here on the beach with his eye of command; this
squelched their insubordination, and at the
sound of the boatswain's whistle they fell in and
listened to Merlin's reprimand. On receiving
their orders, they broke away and scampered like
madmen to the water's edge, where, in the midst
of the tumbling surf, they rolled jovially one
over another wet to the skin, and rolled themselves into the boat amidst imprecations, alas! too
customary amongst these thoughtless men for
them to be at all aware of their impiety.

Poor Frank was still unconscious, but his
messmates had him in their tender care, and
were endeavouring to hoist him aboard in their
arms, wet to the breast; but so unsteady were
they, and with so much ocean-swell on, com-
monly called a ground sea, that the boat was
nigh upsetting and shipping seas several times
by her being bounced against by the unsteady
crew, and thus forced to face the breakers broad-
side, instead of fore and aft or stem and stern;
this caused anxiety to Merlin, who perceived the
danger, and caused him to approach the verge
of the ocean and issue his commands very per-

emptorily. He did so, but they were of no
avail, for the drunken man, coming to conscious-
ness by the wetting from the sea, gave a jerk
and poor Frank was jerked out of his messmates'
hands into the surf. In a moment there was a
cry, "A man overboard;" and there, to Merlin's dismay, was one of his best men being
drawn helplessly out to sea by the out-draught
in the outgoing tide. No time was to be lost;
at the word of command they fell into line, Merlin seaward, the line of men stretching out-
wards until he was up to his arm-pits, when he
grasped the seaman and safely boarded him in
the boat.

Orders were now given for the gig to put
off, steered by Tommy Dart, with Power and
Evered on board, whilst Merlin himself, wet
to the skin, took the command of the boarding
boat and his thoughtless but generous-hearted
men; and in this condition he arrived on board,
and was welcomed by his visitors, who had
arrived before him. Merlin did not mind his
wetting; he gave his orders, and his holiday
crew were now safe and taken care of, and having changed his clothes, he sat down to dinner,
just as the helm was put up and the fore-sheet of

the jib let go and hauled in, which had hitherto held the cutter in irons, or in that position called "lying-to." She now began to feel the force of a strong breeze without resistance, and began gracefully to make a pathway for herself along the ocean, lit up by the glinting moonbeams. The vessel glided majestically along, rising and falling on the waves as she made way.

The dinner was promptly dispatched, indeed it might be more aptly called a hot supper, and the friends now returned to the deck to enjoy the night breeze, as they smoked their pipes and talked over the events of the day and criticized the performances of the wrestlers. They admitted that Jenkins had met with his match, and felt assured that Gundry, the new wrestler, would very soon so distinguish himself as to become the champion of the Cornish ring.

Again and again, as the graceful cutter glided along, was she hailed by the fishermen in their well-manned crafts,—with their tanned-mizen and large square sails set, fishing either with line for cod and ling, or with their large nets for mackerel and other kinds of fish that are of a gregarious nature and swim in shoals,—regarding the result of the match, and whether Jenkins had won the

first prize, as they all took a deep interest in the
wrestling and knew that the cutter's men had been
on shore.   There was a little chaffing when the
fishermen heard from the sailors that Gundry had
won, and were obliged to own that their efforts had
not been crowned with success; but there was
only a little of it, not from the want of will, but
from necessity, as the cutter swiftly glided out of
speaking distance, causing the men to raise the
pitch of their voices moment by moment higher
and higher, until the distance was so much
increased between them that only occasional
words were heard, which were hurried along in
echoes, and then there was silence, broken only by
the ripple of the parting waters breaking on the
copper of the ship or the scream of a disturbed
water-fowl, who had either missed his way home
or found the fascinations of company so powerful
that it had broken loose from its parents' control
in their rocky home, and was, with other unruly
birds of the same feather, making a night of it.

Enjoying themselves on the deck of the cutter,
chatting freely over the events of their lives,
sketching out imaginary plans for their future,
they smoked and drank freely until the hour of
midnight approached and the watch was about

to be relieved, when it was reported they were abreast of the Logan Stone. Power had not seen it; he remembered the one he saw in his own country with Helen, and evinced a desire to see it. Evered lauded the one they were now abreast of to the disparagement of the Irish one so pleasingly alluded to by Power, and so perfectly understood by Merlin. This persistent tone annoyed Power more than usual, he felt he was about to become a member of Evered's family, and felt the impertinence of such egotism and dictation, and especially so after having been a whole day in his company, excited by fatigue and stimulants.

Power having contradicted Evered in his assertions, appealed to Merlin for his opinion, forgetting he had not seen the Irish Logan Rock, which was instantly seized on by Evered for a very sharp and sarcastic remark, "That what the one would say the other would swear to; and although Merlin had not seen the Irish rocking stone, that would not prevent him giving an opinion or a decision on the respective merits of the two rocks." Whilst these remarks were being made, with others of a like character, the drift of the tide had taken the cutter very near the shore,—a position, it may be remarked, she very often assumed in her calling, creeping along, in and out of the many little indentations or bays along the rock-bound coast, where smugglers had their haunts. The celebrated rock in the moonlight now became visible through the night-glass or telescope. Evered felt convinced the Irish rock was but a pebble to this, and stated it could be rocked or logged by the power of an infant, so equably had it been placed in its socket by nature for untold ages. At this moment the watch reported a suspicious movement of a dark form emerging from the shadow of the caves underneath the celebrated stone. On examination it was found to be so suspicious that the orders were given to man the boats and discover the cause of the singular appearance.

Evered, as usual, pronounced the appearance to be smugglers in his judgment, and intimated that there was no time to be lost. Merlin, however, knew better, but he had to be satisfied as to the cause of the singular phenomenon; doubtless he was so in his own mind, but that was not sufficient, he had also to satisfy the curiosity of his crew, and there was only one way, and that was by proceeding to investigate the cause by actual survey, therefore the order to man the boats had been given.

Whatever might have been the cause, whether it was the moon's light shining on the projecting rocks, fashioning them into all kinds of fantastic shapes, or any other, Merlin felt convinced there were no smugglers there, nor life of any kind, creating this phantasmagoria; but, nevertheless, he deemed it his duty to take the command of one of the boats himself, and in doing so he asked his two friends to share his danger, as he humorously invited them to join him in his perilous encounter with men, mermaids, and dragons of the deep. The invitation was accepted, and Power, with Evered, were immediately sitting side by side of Merlin in the boat.

The same caution and silence were enjoined as if there were a certainty of an attack and a necessity for a surprise, but it was very soon discovered that these injunctions were unnecessary as the boats neared the shore, as the singular appearance which had caused so much criticism, and this inspection from the cutter did not move, but only assumed another appearance as it became visible from another point of view, now obtained from the boat from a closer survey. It was now quite apparent that there was no necessity for further investigation as the boat now neared the shore and was on the verge of the ground-swell or breakers, and the cause was now revealed of the fantastic shape from the position of the moon shining on the brow of the beetling rocks.

Evered now pointed to the Logan Rock, almost hanging overhead, reiterated his assertion " that a child might rock it, but not the force of a thousand men could remove it from its socket. No, certainly not; and Merlin and his mathematics, his fulcrum and his levers, and ship's crew to boot, couldn't do it. No, not they!"

" Nonsense!" said Merlin. " Nonsense, Evered; you are talking like a child. Any half-dozen of my crew would heave it out of its socket within half an hour, as easily as they would weigh the ' Sylvia's ' anchor."

Hardly had these words been uttered than the boat was ashore, and the crew bounded out of her without orders and without thinking, heedless from their wrestling and drinking bout, and bounded up the craggy path, yelling all the way, until they reached the summit of the dizzy and hoary granite rocks on which this time-honoured rock was placed. Hardly had Merlin and his companions arrived on the spot, than they perceived by the adroit exertions of the sailors, it was palpably oscillating to and from its very centre.

" Again, lads," shouted Evered. " You are hardly moving it! Rock it more, men, more—harder—more yet !"

Merlin, unconscious of Evered's diabolical intentions, was silently watching the exertions of his sailors, which were increased beyond his cognizance through the energy displayed by Evered, causing an increase of momentum from the thoughtless sailors. In another moment Merlin's attention was drawn to the danger, and before he could check the effect now produced by the vociferations of Evered, who was acting like an excited madman, Merlin and Power to their dismay beheld the huge rock quiver for a second, from the effects of the last push, and then instead of inclining back again to its centre, topple over, but fortunately landwards, causing every man to run for his life, and roll down the precipice many feet below its original position, where it finally settled in a large hollow unbroken by its fall, and removed from its ancient resting-place, where it had been for untold ages an object of curiosity to the tourist, of inquiry to the student of antiquities, and of pride to the county.

The first words uttered by Merlin were, " Oh, Evered, what have you done ?"

" I done !" exclaimed Evered, with well sustained indignation. " Well, I like that. I upset the Logan Rock; why, Merlin, you make me out a giant. Why, it was your crew, man, and surely Evered Trevernen couldn't command them to leave the cutter and commit this act of vandalism."

This taunt provoked into a flame the smouldering passion of Power; he now came between Merlin and Evered, and with withering scorn he ejaculated, " This is an act of a young fiend," and with a blow intensified by uncontrollable anger, he sent Evered howling down the rocks.

" Poor Merlin," said Power, " I understand it all, now."

" I never gave him cause, Power," said Merlin, " but it is my fate. I will call together my men, and we will now, after this beneficent night's work, go on board and get what rest we may, for I shall have to give account of this proceeding, and from what you have heard, Power, you may readily understand how damaging it must be to me."

"But I will bear testimony, my dear Merlin, and so will all your crew."

"Yes, yes, I know, Power, but why were my crew here, at midnight, after the wrestling—drunk it will be said, all drunk. And what can I say? I feel like Michael Cassio—oh, wondrous Shakspeare—my reputation's gone! What, to be duped, to be entrapped and ruined!"

"Eh, ruined," said a voice behind them, trembling with rage and bloody from the blow. "Ruined, say you, and well you may say so. Am I not Evered Trevernen, nephew, and should be heir to my uncle Sir Hugh, and husband of his daughter, my cousin; and have not you Merlin Tregarthen, a no-man's son, crossed my path in every turn of life, ousted me from my uncle's affections, and blighted my dearest hopes in love. Think you that I am not aware of your pretensions,—of your having the audacity to lift your bastard eyes towards Blanche; but I tell you, she was false to me and will be false to you. She prefers Power, and will love him when you are at sea; and oh, bitterest thought of all, Helen is enamoured with you, you cream-faced loon, you bewitched her on the voyage from Ireland, took advantage of her romantic spirit in the storm, fed her soul with outrageous lies of hero-ism and bravery, whilst that poor skunk was too ill to dream or think of treachery. But you are ruined now; you have upset the Logan Rock, the epaulette will be torn from your shoulder and you will be disgraced, Blanche will be delivered from your pretensions, and Helen shall hear no more of your fantastical lies."

These utterances came like thunder-claps in lightning storm on Merlin and Power. They were bewildered—they were in despair—they were for a moment paralysed at the audacity and malignity of Evered. Well it was so, for if the fury of Merlin and Power had found vent Evered must have been murdered; as it was, he gradually greatened the distance as he spoke, and when his last thought found expression, he had disappeared alone, and was lost in the shadow of the rocks. He had done his work; he had shot his arrow, he had calculated the risks; it was now open war between them. Merlin was ruined, Power was a nobody. Time would mend matters, and when things were at their worst they would begin to mend; and with thoughts of this kind, Evered,

alone in the deep night, walked home to Lamorna
House, well satisfied with his day's work, and
ready when the to-morrow would come, to arise
from his bed and proceed to business calm and
collected.

Merlin and Power for a moment misunderstood
each other, but for a moment; for the intentions
of Evered were manifest; still there was a something which Power could not get out of his
mind, so artfully had Evered thrown out the
suspicion of Helen's fickleness, not as it were to
inform him, but to let him know it incidentally by
his accusing Merlin of his breach of trust on
board the cutter, and his unfaithfulness towards
Blanche. This suspicion lasted only for a moment,
for Merlin in his hour of trial evinced nothing
but sincerity.

But it was not Merlin, it was Power who
thought, "Does Helen prefer the romantic sailor
to me?" This thought was now instilled into
his mind, the jealous thought was lodged there,
and Power returned on board with Merlin as sad,
as wretched, and as miserable as he. They looked
on the dislodged rock, they looked on the old site
where ages ago it had been mysteriously placed,
and when the order was given to proceed on

board, they felt their hopes were destroyed which
an hour ago were as settled as the old rock in
its socket, but which was now lying a ruin at
their feet.

# CHAPTER XI.

" They stood aloof, the scars remaining,
   Like cliffs which had been rent asunder;
     A dreary sea now flows between;
   But neither heat, nor frost, nor thunder
     Shall wholly do away, I ween,
   The marks of that which once hath been."

S. T. COLERIDGE.

AFTER a perturbed sleep the Commander of the
'Sylvia' conferred with Power early in the
morning.   He called his men aft, and told them
the consequences of their inconsiderate folly to
him.   To a man they deeply regretted what had
taken place, and swore they would all be revenged
on young Mr. Trevernen if any harm happened
to their Commander, who was not to blame.
Suggestions were made to proceed on shore,
view the scene, and attempt to replace the rock

in its socket, but this was known to be imprac-
ticable, therefore, Merlin determined to put back
to Pendeen, and report the catastrophe truthfully
to the authorities in high quarters. With heavy
hearts Merlin and Power landed from the cutter,
Merlin to forward his ably written report, and
Power to make the best of his way to Tregarthen
Hall, avoiding Lamorna House and the Trevernens.

"Ill news," it is said, "flies apace." The
cutter took some time to sail up to Pendeen with
a light wind, therefore, on Merlin's landing he
found Pendeen up in arms at the sacrilege, with
every imaginable colouring given to the circumstance. One conviction prevailed throughout,
"they were all drunk!" This was a settled belief, and it nearly broke poor Merlin's heart;
another conviction, though not so universal, was
that it was treachery by the subtle Evered, a
diabolical plan of his to ruin Merlin, for most
people had pretty well made up their minds as to
the parentage of Merlin, and consequently the
cause for ill-will and jealousy on the part of
Evered was accounted for, besides, he had grown
a man, and his character for deceit and treachery
was well known, and by many he was detested,

and looked upon as a dangerous man, of whom it was thought he was acting desperately on account of his slighted love by his cousin Blanche. Merlin returned on board with as much haste as possible, and denied access from the shore to his ship until such time as he should hear from the authorities. The returning fishermen from the west brought the news to Pendeen, and carried it rapidly on to St. Keverne, from whence it was carried by 'Dusty,' Blanche's pony, who had been into St. Keverne for letters and ladies' requirements. Sir Hugh himself was the first to hear it, for he met 'Dusty' and his young rider, who was so flurried and big with news that he attracted the attention of the Baronet. Sir Hugh had no occasion to interrogate the lad, for on approaching the Baronet he simply exploded with these words, "They was all as drunk as Fitchers, and they throwed down the Logan Rock last night," and was about to gallop on, forgetful of his customary respect, so excited was he, and so fearful lest he should not be the first to carry the news to the Hall; but the Baronet caught hold of 'Dusty,' and the pony being detained, her rider recovered his self-possession and told the Baronet the news as he had heard it at

St. Keverne, not daring to embellish it, as he
immediately did in the Hall, the kitchen, and the
stables; even Bullock had him into his sanctum
and patted him with cake and a silver sixpence, so
eager and so interested was he to elicit the truth,
which he did pretty well by kindness and severity
mingled in judicious doses. As usual, the ladies
upstairs, who were deeply interested in this matter, were the last to be informed of it; they were
not considered at all, the kitcheners had it all
their own way, and very freely did they speculate
on the consequences one after another as some
thought occurred, again and again laying hold of
young Buttons, and endeavouring to find out
something which they had not obtained through
remissness of persistent inquiry, and exactly did
the cunning young Buttons, who knew he had
only an hour or so for his glory, answer them
until they were crammed with his imagination
and ideas of the matter, which became more
dreadful each time he was questioned, until at
last, when the story reached the stables, Pendeen
was taking vengeance on Merlin, Power, Evered,
and the 'Sylvia's' crew, and they were all in
prison and about to be transported.

At length, to the surprise of all and the dismay

of the young messenger, who now felt he would
be found out and punished for telling such falsehoods, Power arrived at the Hall very flushed
and excited, it was now evident he was not in
prison, so young Buttons got buffeted by the
cook and by Bullock, and had to disappear and
hide his head with 'Dusty' in the stables.
Power without ceremony made his way to the
ladies' boudoir; what would the Abigails give to
be present? but they were prevented, and compelled to live on with their curiosity unsatisfied,
and here we must leave them.   Power told the
story to Helen and Blanche, nor did he refrain
from telling the offensive and distressing observations of Evered; he was unable to, his feelings
had the better of him, and although he felt
Evered's intentions to be most vile, yet he did
not passionately disregard them ; and in repeating
his bitter sentences, he allowed the impression to
be received by Helen that he had not repudiated
them with  sufficient indignation, and  spurned
them with disgust and contempt, but, contrary-
wise, he allowed the feeling to flow into Helen
that although he disbelieved Evered, he allowed
the impression to affect him.   He did not
exorcise it, and this was a living death to the

sensitive Helen, and seen by the less acute
Blanche, who took it up, and exclaimed, " Good
heavens, Power! you don't allow, I sincerely
hope, for one moment, any of these dreadful expressions of Evered to torture you. Think for a
moment how impossible it is for there to be any
truth whatever in them; besides, the Logan
Rock is thrown down, and through his subtle
and malignant agency, and there will be trouble
enough from this cause, without having it intensified by dissensions between us. Oh, Power,
let me implore you to disabuse your mind of any
such unhallowed thoughts, and believe that it is
Evered alone, out of wilful wickedness and spite,
that has caused him to make this mischief; being
miserable himself he makes others so, that is his
happiness. Oh, Merlin, Merlin!" and here poor
Blanche wept bitterly.

Helen immediately sprang to her assistance,
and whilst bending over her with her eyes full
with tears to overflowing, she turned on Power a
love glance that should have melted a heart of
stone, and beheld still, to her dismay, his unsatisfied look, and where was mirrored the expression of his disturbed mind; it made no impression, and was not returned, so absorbed was

he in thought, and so distorted were his affections. Deeply agitated, his mind reeled like the Logan Rock he had just left, and, like it, lost its balance, for he answered the silent appeal by reciting mechanically the charm muttered at the well,—

" Let Blanche and Fred Power inherit the dower;
  Let Helen and Merlin inherit the sterling."

This roused the indignation of Helen, and kindled the fire of anger in her trusting and loving heart. Blanche became insensible and required her affectionate assistance, she gently laid her head on the sofa, looked on her with calm, sorrowful, affectionate pity, and sighed rather than spoke, " Dear Blanche, trust me ;" then rousing all her energies she approached her lover, gazed into his face, pierced his soul with her eagle glance, paused in convulsed agony, placed her trembling hand on her beating bosom, and calmly said, " Power, you have transferred your love ! This dwelling is very beautiful, the mistress very lovely, she is my cousin, but let me assure you she has not transferred her love from Merlin ; you have overlooked that in your calculation when you surveyed the domain. Don't believe it."

"Believe what, Helen?" said Power in anger. "You have said bitter things, which I resent with indignation."

"Do not believe that Blanche will forsake Merlin," coolly said the imperturbable but suffering Helen, "and—"

"And what?" demanded Power very angrily.

"And what!—do you demand what?" said Helen with vehemence, "then I will tell you what,—that she will not forsake Merlin *for you.* That is what I should have spoken had you permitted me to finish my sentence. Oh, Power!" said the half-exhausted girl, "would that I could believe that it was only the wicked observation of my treacherous brother that affects your mind. Reflect! What occasion have I given you for jealousy by my conduct towards Merlin? Think but for a moment how preposterous the thought is that in the storm on the cutter's deck, when Merlin was fully employed in commanding his ship, I could have forgotten you, when you were with me, suffering and ill."

"No, not forgotten me, Helen," Power said with warmth, "but admired Merlin in his romantic and heroic life,—' this is akin to love.'"

"Enough, Mr. Power!—your pretext is suffi-

cient. Our engagement is severed, our intercourse broken, and for ever! I release you; you
are now free to marry Blanche and to forget
Helen Trevernen."

Helen now violently rang the bell. Power,
understanding her meaning, retired before she
could put her impulsive but pardonable intention
into execution, by requesting the domestic to
show Mr. Power the door, and conduct him out
of the room. During this trying scene Blanche
remained on the sofa in a semi-conscious state,
her feelings relieved only by hysterical sobs, until
awakened as from a dream as soon as Power had
left, when poor Helen fairly broke down by her
uncontrollable anguish. Blanche realized the
distressing scene, and not without an effort was
she enabled to compose herself, but seeing her
cousin so prostrate she flew to her and ardently
embraced her.

"Do I dream, Helen?" she said, "am I
bewitched?—have I heard aright? Oh, cousin!
tell me that my brain deceives me,—that I am
under some spell—some hallucination!"

"No, dearest Blanche," said Helen, "you have
heard correctly. Power and I have parted,—our
engagement is severed. He loves you or your

estate—oh, that I must say so!—but it is too true. I never gave him cause for jealousy on board the cutter,—it is a mere pretext, however, instilled into his mind by my dreadful brother. Oh, Blanche, Blanche! I fear Evered—I dread him; he will be the ruin of us all I am convinced, —he is desperate, and bent on doing all the mischief he can to gratify his insatiable revenge."

"Oh, Helen!" said Blanche, now fully conscious and with fortitude, "I am persuaded you are right, and that papa is involved through his artifice and cunning to an extent far beyond his knowledge, and I fear that this upsetting of the Logan Rock was a planned thing, and will be the means of his renewing his wily schemes for our destruction. Poor Merlin, poor lad," she said, "how wretched you are now!—how you are tormenting your mind and destroying your peace with fear that Blanche will blame you! Never, never, Helen, will I forsake him,—I will follow him to the death! But to believe that Power can be so imposed upon! Helen, you are misjudging him, you have misunderstood him; his mind has been abused by Evered,—he cannot have forsaken you!"

"But he has, Blanche," Helen replied, "and

old Kitty's charm has completed his heartless disaffection," and again Helen gave way to tears, and was in turn comforted by Blanche.

Nancy answered the bell of her mistress, bringing in her hand a letter which it is feared had been detained and thoroughly examined downstairs, as far as its outside contents would allow.

" Have you seen Mr. Power?" said Blanche, hardly knowing what she said, so confused was she.

" Yes, my lady, I met him going down the stairs in a very excited state," replied Nancy.

Blanche now took her letter, and Nancy understanding her mistress's manner, said no more; observing she was not wanted, left her to her letter and Helen to her tears. She would have been glad to have rendered assistance to the distressed had she been requested, and with alacrity and feeling, for she no doubt had her own little heart affairs, and could sympathize and would have offered her consolations had she dared, but receiving no further intimation of any need of her assistance or cognizance of her being present, Nancy retired with a tear in her eye, for she knew there was sorrow in both their hearts.

A glass of wine refreshed and nerved to action both Blanche and Helen, and after a sad and solemn conversation, in which they reviewed the circumstances in which they were now placed and the troubles impending, they separately formed their resolutions. Helen, declining all interference on the part of Blanche, announced her determination at once of returning Power's presents, and refusing to see him again, and resolved immediately on returning home, there to dwell with a divided and unhappy household, where discontent and forebodings had taken the place of peace, happiness, and bright and sunny prospects. With this resolve Helen left Blanche, who now read her letter again. It was from Merlin, and by a sure hand; it detailed to her the circumstances of the preceding night, and the wonderful powers of Evered Trevernen, who must have planned, long before he executed this malignant design. It also told her that he should go over to the cottage and confer with his grandmother, for some of Evered's utterances had amazed him, and had bewildered Power so much that he was greatly concerned for him. "He looked, Blanche," it said, "as if Evered had spoken thoughts that were in his mind,—as if the charm chanted at the well had taken a deep hold on his imagination, and was now working, and that fate had destined you for her own. Oh, Blanche!" it also said, "it wounded me sore, and I was struck dumb with awe at Power's countenance,—he looked for all the world like Garrick in 'Macbeth,' when he says, 'Can the devil speak true?'"

Blanche dropped the letter from her hands, and gazed in astonishment on vacancy. A few words escaped her lips as she became more composed, they were—" What a confirmation !"— " How awfully true !"—" I can do nothing for Helen "—"What a conflict last night !"—"What misery now ?" After wiping away the tears that had fallen over her pallid cheek, she took up her letter, saying, " Fear not, Merlin, I will meet you at the cottage; our happiness is in each other's keeping, and nought but death shall separate us !" and then folded it up and placed it, with others from the same beloved writer; and then made her preparations for going with 'Dusty' to the cottage. Blanche felt persuaded that her father had gone over, as he had not returned from his constitutional at his usual hour; she therefore had to estimate the most desirable time for going herself, so as not to meet him there. In this interim of time she called to memory the almost especial affection of her father's kiss last night when the hour of rest had arrived, and her own excessive feelings of reverence and love when she received his customary parental evening blessing, scarcely refraining from tears when he said, " Bless you, my daughter !—my only stay and comfort. May sweet peace abide with you through life !" Well did she call to mind her feelings when she had retired to her sleeping-apartment and abandoned herself to reflection, recalling to memory her dear departed mother as she pictured her in her infancy, and felt more than she had ever before her loss in counselling her in the vicissitudes of life. She was gone, and as she believed to her eternal home of bliss and love, but she remembered her now with a vividness inexplicable, and felt her presence in the precincts of her own soul as she was sitting in deep abstraction and meditation.

Again thought and feeling found vent in expression.

" Oh, my mother !" vehemently Blanche said, " would you were here now for me to pour into your affectionate and sympathizing ear the sorrows of my heart!" And with these depressed feelings she remembered her childhood's prayers, and knew that she was taught to believe that in the day of trouble she was to call on the Author of her being, and that He had promised to deliver her, and to hide her in the secret of His pavilion until the storm had passed. In faith and hope she now commended herself by prayer to His protection, believing that His promises fail not. Refreshed and strengthened from this exercise, she reclined on the sofa, and was soon lulled in sleep, dreaming confused dreams, until the time arrived for her to depart for the cottage and for meeting Merlin, the idol of her soul.

Sir Hugh Laity, after 'Dusty' with his rider had departed, determined on immediately visiting old Kitty. His mind was now in a perturbed state; he knew she had been at work, and was making one final effort to save Blanche, but he was unprepared for the news he had just heard. It never entered into his head to suppose that Evered, if primed and instigated to any overt act, would endeavour to ruin Merlin, but he fully comprehended it now; and this act made him very distasteful to him, it caused him to reflect, and the more he did so, the more uncomfortable he became, for he now saw his cunning and his power. His first thought was to confer with Dr. Fergus, but then he remembered parting with him after his party, and then he could not stomach the Doctor's arbitrary and condemnatory style, and then he knew the Doctor would know all or nothing; and there were certain transactions with Mr. Trevernen of which he was ashamed, and afraid to admit. No, he would go over at once to the cottage, and know the truth from old Kitty; he felt assured she would somehow be in possession of the whole history of the upsetting of the Logan Rock, and he hoped—vain hope!—that the report he had just heard, as usual with St. Keverne reports, had been much exaggerated. With these reflections passing and repassing through his mind, he found himself at the cottage-door, where he was welcomed by old Kitty with all her usual respect. She was prepared to receive him; she had heard the news, and was full of hope and fear,—hope that good results might come, fear that results might accrue altogether unexpected and unanticipated.

"Well, Kitty," said Sir Hugh, "I suppose you have heard what has happened,—ill news travels apace nowadays."

"I have heard the news, my dear master," old Kitty said, "and I fear the boy has deeper designs, and has a bolder spirit, and a more powerful will than I had any conception of. The Logan Rock is thrown down,—that's a fact. And I've heard from one who was present—for the 'Sylvia' has been in port some hours—that Evered's actions were wonderful. His design was not seen through, so well was it planned, brought into execution by his conversation, and accomplished by his intrepidity before poor Merlin had time to reflect. He, poor lad, was taken by surprise, and before he had time to counteract the consequences, the deed was done."

"I believe your account is too true, Kitty," said Sir Hugh; "and from the same source, I suspect, I have further heard that then Merlin, poor lad, upbraided Evered; but he, believing the moment opportune, retaliated by letting out his secret. Power then rushed in, but immediately became lukewarm and confounded, as if the announcement of Helen's preference for Merlin was agreeable, and disclosed that in his mind there lurked a hope for Blanche; this Evered, though bleeding at the mouth, observed, and struck out at the Irishman, calling him all kinds of hard names."

"So the charm works, Sir Hugh," remarked Kitty.

"So I see," replied Sir Hugh; "but, confound the boy! he needn't have upset the old Logan Rock,—the county will be up in arms. What must I do, Kitty? I feel at my wits' end."

"Do," said Kitty, "go to Pendeen, sit in your magisterial chair,—make a fuss. You have done it before, as poor Jenkins well knows; but by-gones are bygones. I would not cast up a thing to vex you now, but old wounds leave their scars behind."

"Oh, Kitty!" said Sir Hugh, "I have abused a chieftain's power, traded on the weak in the madness of a moment, when I ought to have pro-tected and been the honoured. I have mourned, and I am punished. All that man can do I am doing. Oh, I love Merlin as my life, and would that he could marry Blanche."

"Wait patiently, Sir Hugh," said Kitty, "some-thing is done, and I judge I shall soon hear that Miss Helen is in trouble."

"Ah, Kitty," sorrowfully said Sir Hugh, "in causing misery to some, can that make others happy?"

"It is only a change of lovers," cheerfully said

old Kitty, fearing lest her plotting would be thwarted by the remorseful manner of Sir Hugh. "It is not impossible, and once accomplished all would be well."

"But I fear and doubt if your plan will succeed, Kitty," said Sir Hugh in despair.

"Do not doubt," replied old Kitty with great energy, perceiving the state of Sir Hugh's mind, —assuming a defiant manner as the only method of sustaining him in his despair,—"or you may hear to your confusion that my dear young lady and Merlin are married."

"Oh, Kitty, Kitty," said Sir Hugh, with difficulty refraining from tears, "it is impossible; it cannot, must not be,—better let them know at once their real relationship."

"Never, never!" replied old Kitty with assumed fury; "the opportunity for that has long gone by, when you could have told your daughter that Merlin is your son. It is now too late, the hand of destiny was on them when they were betrothed at the well; and now they sother their consciences in the belief that they are cousins, and that Merlin is the natural son of old Sir Evered, and that they are not debarred from wedlock by law nor church. Let them con-

tinue to think so and believe so; but—oh, Sir
Hugh !—keep them ignorant; and if we cannot
succeed in prevention, let them marry, live, and
die in ignorance of their relationship. Now be
patient, and go to Pendeen and investigate the
affair and blame everybody concerned for their
reprehensible conduct."

"I will, Kitty, and screw my courage up to
the sticking-point."

" Do, Sir Hugh, and you will not fail."

Blanche had been hovering about the cottage
for some time, impatient for the departure of her
father. As the lapwing, when disturbed by the
sportsmen, retires from her nest until, the enemy
being foiled, she returns to it, there to indulge
her maternal instinct in the fostering care of her
brood, so did Blanche return to the cottage with
trembling and with fear.

" Is my father gone, Kitty ?" she said. " I
thought he would never go. I have waited
until I am exhausted. Is Merlin here ? Tell
me, have you heard from him ? Oh, Kitty, the
dreadful news is true ; by a sure hand I have
had a letter from him. It is all Evered's doing,
—he is a villain, and has already been the means
of parting Helen from Power. Well you may

start, Kitty. Oh, it is dreadful to contemplate
the wretchedness one wicked man may create!
Would you believe it, dear Kitty, he would separate Merlin from me! and because he cannot
succeed, he endeavours night and day to ruin
Merlin,—hence the upsetting of the old Logan
Rock. I fear the county will be up in arms, and
oh! my dear Merlin will be disgraced."

Old Kitty, immediately on the departure of
Sir Hugh, sat down in her accustomed place,
sad, but knitting as usual when Blanche entered. She expected her, and prepared a reception for her as well as her father. It was a great
trial to this faithful woman to enact her part, she
was prompted again and again to take the sob-
bing girl to her old and weary bosom and tell
her Merlin's history, but she refrained and per-
severed in her part. She was prepared to hear,
although she started when she heard Blanche
say that Helen Trevernen was parted from her
lover. She took courage and commenced a scene
with sternness; she upbraided Merlin for his
want of prudence, and painted with the blackest
colours the saddest picture of the consequences,
and attempted to sow the seed of love for Power
by holding up Evered as her fate. Many im-

patient questions asked by Blanche she now answered by monosyllables only.

"Oh, Kitty," said Blanche, "what could induce Merlin to be so imposed upon and to act so foolishly ?"

"Love," was the only reply vouchsafed.

"Love, Kitty ?" said Blanche, drawing nearer to her and placing her hand tremblingly on her aged shoulder. "What can you mean ?"

"Love and jealousy;" the latter word was now added, and supplemented by "there's never one without the other, Miss Blanche."

"Jealousy ? What do you mean ? I never made Merlin jealous."

"No, never. I wish you had," old Kitty retorted.

"Wish I had, Kitty ? What can you mean ?" said Blanche. "Oh, how bitter you are ! I have done all that honest maid can do to win your affections ; you were wont to pet me and love me, but since poor Merlin and I have foregathered, you have been my bitterest enemy, as if the blood that is in Merlin's veins is not the same as mine, for they say Uncle Evered was his father, and why should he suffer his father's penalty ? Besides, I believe there is the old Norman blood in his veins, which makes him in some way akin to you; and therefore, as you wish Merlin well, there should be no jealousies between us,—but for Merlin's sake, if not for mine, you might at least be kind. Papa will consent to our union at the proper time; he intends it, I am satisfied of it," said Blanche, with an assurance of manner. "And then Merlin will be heir, and the bar sinister pass away in the next generation; and besides, you, who are so well versed in the ancestry of the great, know that many old escutcheons have the cross-bars,—many before and since the Restoration, and that now it has become an honour."

"My old heart is breaking," groaned old Kitty, with difficulty evading argument and rejecting persuasion. Rousing herself to a sense of duty, "It cannot be," she said; "and, by heavens!" she exclaimed, summoning all her strength, and violently getting up from her seat, "it must not be. Merlin is not jealous of you, it is Evered Trevernen, your first cousin, who is jealous and envious of Merlin. He loves you, aspires to your inheritance, will marry you or ruin your father, unless"—

"Unless what, Kitty?" despairingly said Blanche; "unless what, Kitty?" she repeated eagerly.

" Unless you marry Power and Merlin marries Helen," was the chilling reply; " then we may circumvent your cousin and save your father. Think of it, dearest lady. My dearest mistress, there are many reasons for it which you cannot fathom,—it will gladden your father's sad heart, and it will rejoice mine. Time will make you happy, and will show its approval of your sacrifice in its blessings."

" And," sarcastically said Blanche, " will make Merlin wretched, Blanche unworthy of an honest man's love, and a name to be abhorred, and Helen a maniac."

" And Power ?" said Kitty.

" Name him not. But when I forsake Merlin it will be to lie down in despair, and make my bed in the grave."

"Think, my lady ! One word more," said Kitty, " Merlin is in Evered's way; he has thwarted him throughout life, he is now desperate; if love will not lead you to church with him for his bride, he will try and make revenge. Be warned, he is an incarnate villain; but you need not fear him, there is one way of escape from him, and but one. Reflect on what I have said, or you and your house will be consumed like a moth in a flame."

Staggered at such a revelation, Blanche became more and more bewildered, and would have
left the cottage in hopeless misery but for the
arrival of Merlin, whose presence reassured her.
Old Kitty, after receiving the customary tokens of
respect and affection from Merlin, in some measure
departed from her strict line of conduct,—possibly out of kindness, or yielding to her generous
impulses,—she left the sitting-room, without any
attempt at dissimulation, and the lovers had now
an opportunity of conferring with each other,
without the presence of a third party. Merlin
was soon assured that Blanche remained faithful,
and was all his own; but the earnest desire, however, of old Kitty with her reasons was most
distressing when referred to. Both Merlin and
Blanche determined on taking the opportunity
which would presently occur, on old Kitty's return,
of demanding from her, once for all, a full and
explicit explanation for her strange proceedings,
—being fully persuaded she had some over-
whelming and all-paramount reason which di-
rected her, and which she still concealed. They
resolved to let her now understand, be it what
it may, it must be inoperative, as they had fully
made up their minds to brave all circumstances,

and to allow nothing to disturb their engagement. Having settled this point, it was arranged
that Merlin, on finding old Kitty still obdurate
and mysterious, should request her to refrain
from further persecution and allow them to pur-
sue their destiny unmolested. Explanations en-
sued between the lovers regarding Power and
Helen; they compared notes, reasoned with each
other on the strange events they had each wit-
nessed, and still remained without a reason for
Power's conduct and for Evered's actions. Some
great secret remained undiscovered they felt assured, and they believed themselves to be involved in it, for on further reflection, Merlin said
he was convinced Evered was prompted and
guided by some unseen hand, and he believed
it was his grandmother's, who, for some unknown and inconceivable reason, had set him on
to abuse Power's mind, in the hope " he might
forsake Helen and turn his attentions to you, my
dear Blanche," said Merlin, " and you now can
see what effect the charm has had on him."

" Poor Helen !" said Blanche, " I pity her."

" So do I, Blanche," said Merlin; " but I do
not excuse Power, and I feel quite certain he will
very soon be filled with regret and remorse, for

he loves Helen, and she is just the girl to make him happy in his wedded life."

Old Kitty re-entered now, and this prosaic conversation ceased between the lovers, and, as arranged, Merlin attacked his grandmother in the presence of Blanche, but finding her inexorable, he concluded the inquiry by requesting her to cease from troubling and to let the weary rest. Blanche now took a kind farewell of old Kitty, and left the cottage accompanied by Merlin, who walked with her again along the old, old walks, endeared by associations from their earliest childhood, and then, in the old, old way, parted in sorrow and hope,—Blanche for her father's hall, Merlin for his grandmother's cottage.

On their departure old Kitty felt persuaded all her double-dealing was useless, and bitterly she now repented the last step she had taken. She had not broken the engagement between Blanche and Merlin, but, on the contrary, cemented it, and, alas! at the cost of alienating Helen from Power, and perhaps making them wretched and marring their prospects through life. In this frame of mind Merlin found his grandmother on his return. She had been disturbed by the visit from Sir Hugh, perhaps dissatisfied with the advice she had given him in consequence of the influence she had acquired over him, and this aggravated her complaint and made her unusually irritable.

"For what," she said, "should I so deeply interest myself? Let the proud family be humiliated. What have I to do with the Logan Rock? My days of picnic pleasures there are gone with last year's flowers. It is down, let the Laitys follow it. Jenny too, where is she? She has not brought the embrocation from Dr. Fergus. I suppose Jenkins has forgotten it, and so she leaves her old mother. Ungrateful and undutiful daughter! who sheltered you, when in sorrow and distress, from your thoughtless vanity, when you brought disgrace upon my time-honoured name? Yes, soon you'll come full of excuses, but they won't relieve my rheumatism. And now I must hearken to Merlin and hear his story. What! Merlin to be played on like a fife by Evered! But he is a cunning villain, that I know full well, and nothing now will stop him in his career of ruin," and whilst grumbling and complaining, so unlike her self, Merlin approached his grandmother and endeavoured to comfort her. This touched the chords of love, and she now mixed with the severity of her conversation utterances of passionate affection, mingled with scorn at Merlin's having been overreached and overmatched by Evered,—there was sage advice, loving interest, and an expressed determination to use all her influence in his behalf.

Blanche, after parting from Merlin, did not go home, but at a distance followed the steps of her lover. So inconsistent is human life ! Beautiful memories of joyous meetings returned and filled her soul with an intensity of delight; she called to mind that it was here she confessed her love, and admitted Merlin to roam at pleasure in the caverns of her heart; and, as if pleasures are grandest when dangers are nigh, so now her pulse quickened and her heart throbbed with emotion, anxiety, and delight. On nearing the cottage again, Blanche became conscious that she had been dreaming; for as the rose-filled breeze invigorated her and restored her spirits, she experienced a new and an irresistible desire to peep through the latticed window and see Merlin when he was not thinking of her,—when he was in earnest talk with his grandmother,—perhaps so necessary to him for his guidance. " Would she interrupt the conversation and discover herself? No, not for worlds. What would old Kitty think of her, and what would Merlin?"

And so, half-terrified, she continued gazing through the window, and saw old Kitty in her anger bending her angry brow on Merlin in one moment, and in another worshipping him with an adoring gaze of love. What passed Blanche knew not; she did not wish to know; she had come to the old cottage well to drink of the still waters, if she could find them; she drank instead her fill of the troubled. She had now seen Merlin when he was unconscious of her presence, and had seen with her own mortal eyes the admiration and love of old Kitty for her grandson. She had now drunk her fill of the sweet but troubled waters of hope, courage, and consolation; and, like a timid fawn that had quenched her thirst at the rippling stream, startled at the rustling leaf and frightened with the mirror of her own self, flies off to the sheltered forest, so Blanche flew with quick and quickening steps along the dear old wooded paths, and found herself at shelter in her home beloved.

The event of the Logan Rock had become history at the Hall. All were more or less inter-

ested in the event, down to Nancy, the lady's
maid, who had her lover on board the ' Sylvia.'
The festivities were now broken in upon, all
were estranged,—Helen had left for Lamorna
House, Power had left to engage a post-chaise,
as the General had now determined on leaving
at once for London, and posting up direct. The
early part of the evening at the Hall was a very
dull one ; Blanche did not make her appearance,
nor Mrs. Power, but busied herself in preparations for leaving on the following day. Merlin,
on his way over to the Hall, met Power, now
very cast-down and sorrowful, for the sudden
determination of the General to leave at once for
London discomposed him sadly. He was glad to
see Merlin, and frankly told him he had said
adieu to the Hall, that he had not seen Blanche,
that it appeared to him he was shunned by her,
and he regretted he had not been allowed an
opportunity of sending one kind word to Helen.
This led to Merlin making an observation on his
extraordinary conduct, and asking him plainly
whether he had seriously considered the charm
chanted by old Kitty at the well.

Power was an impulsive but an honest man,
and he frankly owned to Merlin that ever since he

had known him there had been so much of mystery about his life that he was puzzled, and when Evered spoke as he did he was astonished; but he reiterated with passion, again and again, that the breaking off his engagement with Helen was her fault,—she never considered his feelings nor his temptation, but aroused every faculty of her fiery intellect to see if she had any ground for her suspicion.

"This maddened me, Merlin," Power said; " if she had only borne with me, and reasoned with me, she would have discovered that I had not ceased to love her, that I was not in love with Tregarthen estate, but that I was in perplexity. However, we have parted; I think Helen is over-hasty, and will regret her precipitancy; but to be rid of the companionship of her brother and have nothing more to do with Mr. Trevernen is, I grant, a relief.

"I believe we shall go to Ireland soon, the General has had enough of Cornwall. He likes Sir Hugh, but he detests Mr. Trevernen, and is happy to escape his incessant importunities for mining speculations and money borrowing; he thinks also that house of business will soon come to the ground, and he fears poor Sir Hugh will tumble with it. If such is the case, the estate after all is not so valuable; but for the sake of Blanche and her father and you, I hope the Trevernens will not involve Tregarthen in ruin.

"I can hardly expect, Merlin, that we can become correspondents, but I now only will say that a letter under cover to the General, addressed to the Hon. East India House, in London, will find me sooner or later. When these troubles are over, and I hope they will be, think of Fred Power kindly, and he will often and often do the same of Merlin Tregarthen."

The young men now parted, each convinced they would eventually see each other again,— Merlin thinking better of Power, and determined to let his thinkings be known, in the latent hope that Helen would be one day reunited to him, although he scarcely dare cherish the hope when he considered the detestation of the Powers for the Trevernens, and their conviction that ere long they would be ruined.

Merlin obtained an interview with Blanche. She told him Power had gone, but that she declined seeing him and saying good-bye; Merlin told her that he had met him, and told her all that had passed. Power was not free from blame or doubt in Blanche's estimation, but she thought her fiery cousin had been quite severe enough. Power had said nothing to her.

"True, he waited," she said, "for our quarrel, dear Merlin, to come off, and then I should have had him at my feet. He had no objection to change partners, but it was not his proposal, you see, dear, it was only proposed to him, and it found a lodgment in his brain, not in his heart; and therefore I forgive him, and have told Helen so, but she will not brook rivalry, it is not with her,—if there is no Blanche, Helen will do. No, dear Merlin, Helen must shine in the same orbit as Blanche."

"And as brilliantly," said Merlin.

"I pity her sufferings," said Blanche, "for there is wounded pride as well as forsaken love, with the awful addition of a despondent household at Lamorna House."

"Do you know, Merlin," continued Blanche, "I overheard our kitchen folk talking, and I was surprised at their freedom, and their opinion of Uncle Trevernen. If what they say is true, he is not respected as a great merchant; and they expressed sympathy for papa, as if he had been cajoled. I fear the good folks are busying them-

selves about the Trevernens; but I do hope papa
is not very much involved with them.  I am certain he is to some large extent, for that horrid
Marsh, papa's man of business, is so often here
now, and he makes papa fretful and sad.

" And now, dear Merlin," she inquired, " what
further news about your trouble ?  I do not
think after all you will be affected much,—it will
be a nine days' wonder.  You must be very kind
to papa this evening, and humour him as much
as possible ; he will talk about the affair and will
use his influence.  He is in better spirits, I am glad
to say ; the 'Hercules' is in Falmouth harbour,
wind-bound,—the splendid frigate to memory
dear,—oh, those happy evenings under the spangled sky !  Papa has sent off a messenger, and I
expect the Commander will be here, and he will
help us, I am sure."

Armed with this love-advice, Merlin spent a
consolatory evening with Sir Hugh.  As the
evening drew on, Mrs. Power appeared, accompanied with Blanche, in the drawing-room ; it
was the last evening, there were no unpleasant
allusions, and it—like others—passed away.  The
Powers left on the following morning, Merlin
also for sea, Blanche was again alone, and Sir

Hugh at Pendeen on magisterial duty. He however did not, in old Kitty's language, make a
fuss; a kind brother-magistrate, who knew Merlin and esteemed his qualities, suggested to Sir
Hugh the propriety of his remaining quiet. He
took the advice and profited by it, for the Lords
of the Admiralty, through the influence of the
Commander of the 'Hercules,' absolved Merlin
from blame, and he was restored to favour, under
the one condition that he should replace the Rock
in its former position, to which command he
readily consented. He had every kind of help in
tackle of extraordinary quality, granted from the
dockyard, and very soon, by the adroit management of the skilful magistrate, the people forgot
all about the upset of the Rock, and were deeply
interested in the skill and success of the 'Sylvia's' crew in replacing it. Such is life! There
was, however, one exception—a strange one—
and from a quarter the least expected; he was,
although beloved and respected, a cynic and a
grumbler,—it was Dr. Fergus. He could not
forgive or forget the vandalism; if he could have
the Rock and its belongings blown a thousand
miles away into millions of fragments, he would
have been content. Not so now; there was the

Rock, just as it was before, not a vestige of ma-
chinery left,—nothing to show that it had been
interfered with. It would log or rock,—some
enthusiastic friends said better than before,
whilst others, more prejudiced, maintained that
it wouldn't rock at all, it only oscillated; but not
being able to explain their distinction, they settled down into a party of discontented antiqua-
rians, of whom Dr. Fergus was the leader. He
lectured at the Institution on Druidical remains,
Druidical rites, sacrifices, etc. *ad nauseam*; but he
was quietly allowed by the skilful magistrate to run
himself out, which in time he did, after provoking
fun and jokes with the men folk, and horror and
fainting with the women folk, at his horrible descriptions of the ancient mode of offering up holo-
causts (a very favourite word with the Doctor) of
human sacrifices. Time, however, has beaten the
Doctor; it began beating him when he left off
lecturing, it continued to beat him when he forgot to make it the chief source of conversation
and lamentation of the follies and barbarities of
the age, and it finally beat him when he did
nothing more than grunt when, in after-years,
the circumstance was alluded to in his presence.
Nevertheless, he has never been known to visit

the Rock since the catastrophe, and when asked the locality or any information concerning it, which he is sometimes, and occasionally unnecessarily so, he either disdains to give the information or affects entire ignorance of such a rock being in existence. The Rock, however, is in its old place, and continues to be visited by the curious, and regarded as a wonderful ancient phenomenon, although it was disowned by the worthy antiquary, who for many years has been mouldering in his grave in St. Keverne church-yard.

END OF VOL. II.

PRINTED BY TAYLOR AND CO.,
LITTLE QUEEN STREET, LINCOLN'S INN FIELDS.

www.ingramcontent.com/pod-product-compliance
Lightning Source LLC
Chambersburg PA
CBHW021045030726
47496CB00006B/1692